WOMEN

Women

MIHAIL SEBASTIAN

Translated from the Romanian by Philip Ó Ceallaigh

Other Press · New York

Originally published in Romanian as *Femei* in 1933
English-language translation copyright © Philip Ó Ceallaigh 2019

Production editor: Yvonne E. Cárdenas
Text designer: Jennifer Daddio / Bookmark Design & Media Inc.
This book was set in Goudy Old Style, Bernard Fashion, and Bernhard Gothic
by Alpha Design & Composition of Pittsfield, NH

1 3 5 7 9 10 8 6 4 2

LIBRARY OF CONGRESS CATALOGING-IN-PUBLICATION DATA

Names: Sebastian, Mihail, 1907–1945, author. | Ó Ceallaigh, Philip, translator.
Title: Women : a novel / Mihail Sebastian ; translated from the Romanian
by Philip Ó Ceallaigh.
Other titles: Femei. English
Description: New York, NY : Other Press, 2019.
Identifiers: LCCN 2018028486 (print) | LCCN 2018035268 (ebook) |
ISBN 9781590519554 (ebook) | ISBN 9781590519547 (paperback)
Subjects: | BISAC: FICTION / Coming of Age. | FICTION / Contemporary Women. |
FICTION / Cultural Heritage.
Classification: LCC PC839.S37 (ebook) | LCC PC839.S37 F4613 2019 (print) |
DDC 859/.332—dc23
LC record available at https://lccn.loc.gov/2018028486

Renée, Marthe, Odette

✿

ONE

t's not yet eight. Stefan Valeriu can tell by the sunlight, which has crept only as far as the edge of his chaise longue. He can sense it climbing the wooden legs, feel it caressing his fingers, his hand, his naked arm, as warm as a shawl...More time will pass—five minutes, an hour, an eternity—and a flickering blue light with vague silver streaks will appear through his closed eyelids. Then it will be eight and perhaps time to start thinking about getting up. Just like yesterday, and the day before that. But he'll remain lying there, smiling at the thought of this sundial he constructed on the first day, using a chaise longue and a patch of terrace. He passes his hand over his sun-scorched hair, rough as hemp fiber, and accounts it no great loss in the end that he's forgotten his bottle of Hahn oil—his sole extravagance, but a precious one—in his room on the rue Lhomond in Paris. He enjoys passing his fingers through tangled hair that received no more than a cursory brushing that morning, and its roughness tells him how blond it has become.

It must be very late. Just now, he heard the sound of voices from the pathway. Somebody, a woman, shouted

WOMEN

from down at the lake. Perhaps the Englishwoman from
yesterday, the one he'd watched swimming powerfully. He
had been surprised by the way she struggled with the water;
she seemed to know only the breaststroke.

Stefan swings his leg over the edge of his lounger and
feels about the grass with his naked foot for a patch of
dampness. He knows that somewhere not too far to the
left, toward the hedge, is a place that holds the dew until as
late as lunchtime. There it is. His body, baking lazily in the
heat, and the feeling of that cold vegetation.

On Monday evening, going downstairs to the guesthouse dining room—he had just arrived at the station
after a long journey and had hurriedly changed his shirt—
the talkative Serbian woman at the table at the back announced, for all to hear:

—*Tiens, un nouveau jeune homme!* . . .

Stefan had been doubly grateful. For the *nouveau* and
for the *jeune homme*. He had felt old a week earlier, on his
way out of his final medical exam, and weary. Tired after
the sleepless nights, the mornings at the hospital, long afternoons in the library, and the two-hour exam in a dim
hall before a deaf professor who was dressed for winter and
whose collar appeared to be dirty . . . And then the name of
this Alpine lake, stumbled upon on a map in a bookshop,
the train ticket bought at the first travel agency he'd come
across, the trip through big stores to buy a white sweater,

gray flannel trousers, and a summer shirt. And then a journey that was like an escape.

Un nouveau jeune homme.

✦

Stefan doesn't know anybody. He's been greeted in passing
a few times but has not let himself be drawn out. His accent
makes him coy; he is not eager to give himself away as foreign on the first day. He passes between the tables after
lunch, aloof, with the trace of a frown. Perhaps he seems
gruff. But it's just laziness.

Above, behind the terrace, the forest begins. There's
a small clearing there with dense, long, yielding grass. He
crushes it beneath the weight of his sleepy body all afternoon and the next day finds that it has sprung back completely, as though it had never been touched. He throws
himself down, arms spread, legs stretched out, his head
buried in the vegetation. He succumbs to what is forcing
him down, though he wishes he could fight it.

A squirrel has leaped from one hazel to another.
How do you say squirrel in French? There's an immense
silence...No. That's not true. That's an expression from
books. There's an immense racket going on, an immense
animal hubbub, crickets chirping, frantic grasshoppers,
and the clink of the carapaces of beetles as they collide

in midair and plummet earthward like beads of lead. In all this, the sound of Stefan Valeriu's own breathing is one more detail, one more little expression of life, no more trivial or essential than a squirrel leaping or that grasshopper perched on the toe of his boot, believing it to be a stone. It's good to be here, an animal, a creature, a nobody, sleeping and breathing on a two-meter patch of grass under a common sun.

If it felt like thinking, how would a cricket think about eternity? And if that eternity had the savor of this afternoon... Below, on the guesthouse terrace, chairs and shawls and white dresses can be seen. And beyond, the idyllic, clear, blue lake. A postcard.

TWO

Through the cool blue light of evening, muffled sounds come across the lake, from the town, from beyond the distant electric lights. It's Thursday, and a military band is playing in the municipal park. Almost everybody in the guesthouse has gone there, taking the 8:27 boat, to attend. Stefan Valeriu has remained. The whole valley, spread out before the terrace, is suffused with deep blue.

—Do you play chess, sir?

—Yes.

Why did he say "yes"? It would have been so simple to say no, and then he'd be outside, free to continue his stroll upon the terrace. A hasty "yes," and now he's in the common room, in front of a chessboard, condemned to concentrate. His opponent is a tall, bony, swarthy, middle-aged man who plays slowly and methodically.

—You didn't go to the concert.

—No.

—Me neither. My wife was dead set on it, so I let her. But me...

Stefan has lost a rook, but on his left flank he has constructed a focused attack on the king.

—Are you from the Midi?

—No. I'm Romanian.

—Impossible! You sound like a Frenchman. Or maybe it's just that I'm not used to the accent here. Because I'm not from France either. I'm Tunisian.

—Tunisian?

—Yes. Well, French from Tunisia. I have plantations there. Marcel Rey's the name.

Stefan's attack has failed, and, having left himself wide open, he loses the game. In the meantime, the concert-goers are returning. Hearing the whistle of the boat from the jetty, they go out to await them. Many lively voices, exclamations, handshakes, noisy greetings.

—Oh Marcel, if you knew how lovely it was...

—Renée, please meet a new friend. My wife.

She is a tall, slender woman. In the dim light, only her eyes can be seen. Stefan kisses her hand. A small, cold hand, like any other.

⚘

They've been on a little excursion to Lovagny to see a castle. The three of them—Marcel Rey, his wife, and Stefan. And Nicole, the Reys' little girl. They've walked about a lot, laughed, and taken photographs. Monsieur Rey has a small movie camera and sometimes films scenes which he then sends to Paris to be developed.

—Renée, go over there with Monsieur Valeriu. Farther, into the light. That's it, laugh, talk, a bit of action.

—If we're in a movie, Madame, Stefan whispers, then make it a love story.

He says it casually. He is sufficiently offhand for it to pass as a joke, if required.

Renée smiles quizzically, and says nothing. Stefan plays with Nicole's curls. Monsieur Rey films it all.

✍

He knows their entire story. They were both born in a small town in Tunisia and are from old colonial families. He came to France only once before, in 1917, took a bullet in the shoulder after two hours in the trenches, and was back home within a week of leaving. This is the first time she has gone farther than Tunis. They married in 1920, had a child—Nicole—in 1921, bought a vineyard in 1922, a plantation the following year, and a couple more each year thereafter. Their town, Djedaida, is fifty kilometers from Tunis. It's a small European settlement, surrounded by native tribes that gather on the outskirts whenever there's a bad drought and wander the little streets looking disaffected. During those periods, the Reys sleep with a gun under their pillow. On Saturday evenings, when the plantation workers are paid, Renée stands by the telephone, in case it's necessary to call to Tunis for help.

She narrates all this quietly, matter-of-factly. She's a little bit tired and Stefan Valeriu has to ask three questions to receive one answer.

—Can you hand me my shawl from over there? I'm cold.

He throws it over the chaise longue and, in arranging it over her, his hand happens to linger on her knee. She starts with fright and shouts, senselessly, "Nicole, Nicole!"

※

In the evening, Stefan replies to some letters from Paris. "I haven't met anybody. Just a family of Tunisians, him a good chess player, her a virtuous wife. I don't think they're happy together."

※

He's taken a boat from the guesthouse's jetty, rowed to where the lake opens out and the view of the steep valley in the mountains looks symmetrical, dropped anchor, and flopped down on the bottom of the boat, with the oars dangling in the wavelets. Lazy and without a care, floating in the vast emptiness. He closes his eyes. He is engulfed by sunlight.

Earlier, in the common room, he again saw the young couple who recently arrived at the guesthouse and have taken the room situated on its own, across from the main building. A honeymoon, probably. She's impressive. She had entered shyly, her eyes and the hint of negligence in her attire suggesting to Stefan that she'd spent a torrid night. The aroma she left behind seemed to fill the entire building. An aroma redolent of a sensual nest with warm pillows, and a sleepy female body you find yourself making love to in the gentle morning light.

— It's intolerable! It's contagious! There should be a law against it! says Stefan aloud, to himself. In reply, a wavelet slaps the boat, a distant swimmer shouts something, and in the town the clock of the church of Saint-François-de-Sales strikes ten.

THREE

There is an intriguing couple over in a quiet corner of the terrace. He has only noticed them today, but perhaps they have been around for some time. She is not yet old and there is something glorious about her beauty. She's perhaps thirty-five. Perhaps older. Tall, calm, with strong features, and a smile that isn't a smile, but is the general repose of her face. The man she's with is just a boy. He looks hardly twenty. He's sitting on the grass by her chair and speaking quickly, animatedly, with jerky gestures. She half-listens to him, and slowly passes her fingers through her hair.

Her lover? Husband? A gigolo? A bit of each, Stefan thinks, surprised by a surge of jealousy, perhaps of humiliation, that he, a vigorous young creature of twenty-four, rested and alone, is waiting for something to appear around the corner. But it does not come.

—Do you want to sing a song, Nicole?

—Yes.

✿

It's very late. Everybody has gone to bed. Stefan Valeriu is left waiting alone on the terrace.

—Young man, sleep is better than the stars, Monsieur Vincent, a fat, jolly man from Marseille, called out to him earlier.

He didn't reply. After dinner, the woman and her young companion had gone down to the lake. They still haven't returned. For a while, Stefan observed their stroll down the jetty: her pale shawl, stirring in the breeze, and his white sweater were easily visible. Now nothing can be made out, but the night is vast and they will have to return.

⁀ℛℴ

A powerful shudder. A boat has collided with Stefan Valeriu's. He sits up, surprised.

—Who's that?

—Me.

It's the young companion. He laughs awkwardly, as though pleased to meet Stefan, while apologizing for the accident.

—I was rowing facing the wrong way and didn't notice you there. It's my first trip on the lake. How's the water?

—Fine.

—Do you swim?

—I do.

—Mind if I drop anchor here myself?

—Go ahead.

Stefan has lain down again at the bottom of the boat, set on being unsociable. The youth lies in his boat, dangling his feet in the lake, splashing bright beads of water in the sunlight.

Stefan Valeriu whistles.

—"Bolero"?

—Yes.

He goes quiet again. The youth whistles the tune that Stefan began. Up on the distant guesthouse terrace, a white dress moves like a flag in the breeze.

—*Hallo, hallo!*

The youth waves enthusiastically. He receives a more measured wave in return.

—You were saying you swim, says Stefan, irritated by this romantic exchange.

—Yes, I do.

—Let's have a race then. To the farthest jetty and back three times, no stopping. The loser has to go into town for cigarettes. I've left mine in my room.

He wants to win. He knows that what he's doing is stupid, silly, and mean, but he wants to humiliate the youth, to wreck his idyll. The youth accepts the challenge. For a moment they both stand erect in the sunlight like twin swords... They've dived.

He could let him get ahead for a few moments, give him false hope, and then surge forward in a couple of strokes, coming level and then overtaking him. But no. It has to be a clear, total, crushing defeat, from start to finish. Stefan is well ahead. The young man is struggling. He can hear him panting, his rhythm slackening, and then turning onto his back to breathe and rest. He's ahead by five meters. Ten. An infinity. He's won. His opponent is far behind. The bell for lunch rings out from the guesthouse. The youth finally catches up. Stefan helps him onto the boat. He looks grave.

—That's the lunch bell. Mama will be annoyed.

—Mama?

—I promised to be back in time.

—The woman in white?

—Yes.

—Why didn't you say she was your mother?

—You didn't ask.

Stefan says nothing. He can't think of anything to say. He feels like hugging the youth, but there's no time. He rows quickly, with one arm and then with the other, because at the same time he is removing his swimming shirt, drying himself off, getting dressed. At the shore, he ties up his boat sloppily on the jetty and helps the youth to secure his boat.

—Come on!

He grabs his arm and runs without looking back. The slope up to the guesthouse is hard work. The midday sun beats down. Still. There is no time to waste.

—Let's take a break.

—No. What's your name?

—Marc. Marc Bonneau.

At the entrance to the guesthouse, that white dress. She is waiting. Stefan sees her and stops two paces from her, surprised that they are standing face to face. Standing before this composed woman, he is suddenly embarrassed to realize that his hair must be tousled, that he's sweating and his collar not properly buttoned.

—Madame, I beg your pardon. Marc is late because of me.

—Very bad. Two hours of detention each. And no water during lunch. Look how you've perspired.

She takes his handkerchief from his shirt pocket and wipes his brow with it.

—See?

꙳

The evenings are long and monotonous. Monsieur Rey, Monsieur Vincent, and Marc Bonneau play cards. Marthe Bonneau and Renée Rey converse. Stefan Valeriu, seeking sanctuary behind the open covers of a book, smokes.

—Monsieur Valeriu, Nicole went to bed a long time

ago. It's way past bedtime for children. You should follow her example.

—Just a little later, Madame Bonneau. I'll go when I've finished this chapter.

—Oh, children these days...

Everybody laughs. Except Stefan, who appears absorbed by his book and raises an eyebrow, indicating that he is present and yet not.

—This Monsieur Valeriu, growls Monsieur Vincent, is a sick man. A couple of nights ago I caught him on the terrace talking to the stars. This morning he didn't go out onto the lake, and now look at him—he says nothing and doesn't get annoyed. Sure signs, by God...

—Please leave him be and don't bother him. Am I not your guardian here, Monsieur Valeriu?

—Indeed, Madame Bonneau!

He looks straight at her, with an innocent, acquiescent smile that gives him the interior freedom to observe and imagine. Is she hiding nothing, this very beautiful woman? Her big, well-formed eyes rarely blink and see well. No moments of vagueness, no shadow of melancholy. Sometimes when she passes Stefan she lays her hand on his shoulder, a gesture she repeats a minute later with Marc. She's at ease, possibly because she knows she is protected; protected by her maturity, by the presence of her son, by the grave composure of her beauty.

—Will your game keep Marc much longer?

—Until we're finished...

—Fine, but who am I to take my evening walk with?

—With young Valeriu.

—Really? Would you accompany me, Monsieur Valeriu?

—If I'm allowed out at this late hour, Madame Bonneau...

—Indeed, it's late for you. But we'll make an exception this evening. Will you join us, Madame Rey?

—I won't. I'm afraid it's rather cold down at the lake at this hour.

They go together down the pathway to the gate of the guesthouse, toward the lakeshore. Having stepped outdoors, they are suddenly silenced, surprised by the vastness of the night, something which couldn't have been guessed at inside, in the common room. They can hardly see, but each feels the presence of the other from the sound of their sandals on the pebbles. As they get closer to the lake, the night opens out, as though illuminated from within the body of water itself, by lights ranging from blue to green. A vague murmur issues from all along the lakeshore, perhaps the rustling of the forest or the lapping of the waves upon the shore, as steady as a pulse, from the sleeping plants, from the rocking of a boat that has floated loose from the jetty. Madame Bonneau has taken Stefan Valeriu's arm, and not in a halfhearted way. On the contrary, her grip is firm and assured, and without any note of sensuality.

—Madame Bonneau, I want to tell you, you're very beautiful.

—And very old.

—Perhaps. But above all beautiful.

A long silence.

—And?

—And, that's all!

From time to time an automobile passes, throwing a cone of harsh light on their faces before disappearing around a bend, leaving them feeling a little awkward, as though a stranger had entered a room while two people were having a private conversation. Stefan Valeriu notes this first moment of embarrassment and counts it among his victories.

🙢

Marthe Bonneau is staying on the first floor, at the far end of the guesthouse grounds. From his second-floor room on an oblique wing of the building, Stefan surveys her window without arousing suspicion. He has seen her just now, after breakfast, leaving her group of friends on the terrace and entering her lodgings. She stopped in her doorway and waved back at them—a wave of tiredness or sleepiness. Then she opened her window and her porcelain arms flashed briefly in the sunlight as she let her shutters down.

Stefan made his move without pausing to reflect on what he was doing or risking. He took the stairs quickly, strode across the garden and rapped on her door, and didn't pause for her response. He'll say the first thing that crosses his mind, doesn't matter what.

—Is Marc here?

—You know he isn't. He's in Grenoble. Didn't you accompany him to the station yourself yesterday?

—Well…

—Well then, come on inside, since that's what you're here for!

She's reclining on a sofa by the window, an unopened book in her hand. She seems unsurprised by his visit.

—Come here and sit down.

Stefan's hand goes automatically to his collar, as though to straighten an imaginary tie. It's curious how her presence always makes him feel improperly or negligently attired and inadequate before her studied, calm simplicity. He is bothered in particular by a lock of hair that he tries to tame but that always falls over his forehead. It makes him feel that he must look unkempt next to her tidy beauty; that she must dislike this about him.

—I was watching you a little earlier, before lunch, when you were swimming. I was on the shore with Renée Rey and we both enjoyed the sight. You swim beautifully.

—Madame, I came to speak to you about another matter entirely.

He'd like to take her hand in his, suddenly, in order to clarify matters, but he is uncertain whether he should act on the impulse, and this makes him pause in his speech also. He hesitates. She looks at him with the same protective smile and, with the most relaxed air she takes his hand in hers, as though to say, Look, it's very simple, you shouldn't torture yourself over such trifles.

—Look, here comes Renée Rey. Madame Rey, won't you keep us company? Then, to Stefan: I like this woman. Just as I like Marc, and I like you. All three of you are young and that's lovely to behold, for someone like me, who is past all that.

※

She has invited him along with her on a Sunday morning visit to a nearby village where there is a church with curious eighteenth-century stained glass windows that they had noticed when passing through on a previous occasion. She's wearing a long, black, high-cut dress and a wide-brimmed hat, which makes her composed features calmer still. She's leaning against a central column, with Stefan to her right and Marc to her left, both in their holiday clothes.

Imagining how his group would look from a distance, Stefan Valeriu suddenly feels like a decorative detail in a predetermined tableau. This church, deliberately chosen, the two old women on their knees nearby, Madame Bonneau's austere dress, their open collars, the cool air beneath the cupola ...

—*Maman, que tu es belle*, Marc whispers.

For the first time, Stefan regards her with hostility, without actually raising his eyes to her, for fear of disturbing the pose. He watches her out of the corner of his eye, from his simulated attitude of ease. How this woman must have chosen the exact place to stop, the column she would happen to lean against, the hand that would stay half-covered, because the act of unbuttoning her glove would be surprised by the pipe organ and abandoned! How she must have premeditated the way her head is tilted slightly back, how her lower lip is relaxed, no more able to continue smiling, the slight flaring of her nostrils...

Maman, que tu es belle!

Madame Bonneau responds to Marc by resting her hand on his shoulder. The other hand then rests on Stefan's shoulder, for symmetry.

In a moment, he is tempted by the thought of breaking up the group. A surge of indignation. He shifts slightly, imperceptibly, to the right, and her hand, momentarily unsupported, falls.

⚜

It is the third day of Stefan Valeriu's tactical withdrawal. Since the incident in the church, he has met with Marthe Bonneau only in company. The evening joke has ceased to function.

—Monsieur Valeriu, Nicole has gone to bed. Children should be tucked in by now.

—You're right, Madame. It's late.

He stood up, put out his cigarette, closed his book, and politely wished them all a good night. Her eyes sought his several times. When he chanced to meet them, he looked away with that same apologetic gesture you make when you find you have unwittingly glanced at a letter someone was writing. She has asked him on several occasions to join her on a local excursion, and Stefan has declined decorously, offering entirely plausible reasons.

—I'm terribly sorry, Madame. I promised some friends in Aix—you remember, my Romanian friends, the ones I met last Saturday on the lake?—promised I'd take a trip to see them. If I could telephone them, it would be simple. But a telephone, in this wilderness...

Stefan Valeriu has some experience of the power of such polite rebuffs. He tells himself that Madame Bonneau's confident facade will eventually crumble in the face of them. Small signs of irritation are visible: a trace of being offended in her smile, the abrupt way she puts on and takes off her gloves, a forced indifference in her speech. Just now, after breakfast, as they rose and moved outside in random groups, Madame Bonneau, whom Renée Rey had engaged in a discussion that looked as if it would take some time, sought his eyes and tried to signal to him to wait, that she wished to tell him something. But he, busy filling his pipe, judged he could afford to ignore such a discreet appeal. He loped away slowly and headed upward toward the woods and his usual place. Madame Bonneau watched him in agitation, not knowing how to make her request explicit because of Madame Rey, who was speaking animatedly. In feigning incomprehension, Stefan had adopted his most innocent expression. Now, in this hidden place, he relives the scene and savors all the details, maliciously. He laughs openly, immodestly: he has won.

At last, Marthe Bonneau is on her own. She looks out past the terrace railings for a sign of him, spies him, maybe, and sets off toward the woods. Stefan hears her dress rustling against the vegetation. Lying as he is in the grass, he digs his fingers into the earth, to be sure of his self-control.

—I'll wager, Madame Bonneau, that you're just passing through by chance.

—You lose the bet. I came to see you.

A plain and simple answer, without artifice. Stefan Valeriu's irony hangs uselessly, like the tension in somebody who has gone to unlock a door with a skeleton key, only to find it open. Her reply—like a single chess move—has invalidated a victory striven for over three days.

—May I sit beside you?

He is stretched out on the grass. She sits, leaning back against a hazel tree, dominating him by the simple act of looking down at him. Stefan feels how evocative this arrangement is—perhaps accidental—of her attitude of watchfulness and his of freedom and indifference. And he laughs, not knowing if her aptitude for finding the most poised and dignified pose is deliberate or instinctive. But it's all the same in the end, whether it's conscious or instinctive. Her superior vantage is the source of her incontestable beauty. A beauty even clearer in this afternoon sunlight.

—No doubt about it, Madame Bonneau. You're very beautiful.

—No, my dear friend. Very calm, that's all. Though sometimes they're the same thing.

—Now, for example ...

—No. Because I'm certainly not calm now. Because I'm leaving tomorrow!

Stefan doesn't trust himself to speak. He fears he might get to his feet if he begins. He closes his eyes and waits.

—I'm leaving tomorrow and I wonder if I haven't stayed too long already. A moment too long.

—Meaning?

For a moment she doesn't speak, and no shadow falls over her cheek, which Stefan, who is gazing at it, would like to see devastated by the pain of repressed longing. The same self-assured expression, the same symmetrical features framing that vigilant smile.

—Meaning?

—Meaning, the way you walked across the terrace this morning in a white shirt, with an open collar. Your foreign name, that nobody in the guesthouse knows how to pronounce. Your earnest, confused youthfulness, your still unlived life, the foreign newspapers you get sent from afar, the letters that arrive for you with their strange stamps. Your gruff, unsociable exterior, your bursts of enthusiasm, your passion for books and lounging in the grass. It's all very appealing.

Stefan seeks her hand and kisses it, but all he encounters is a woman who is so calm, so self-assured, and just surprised by his cold grip, that he can neither drop her hand, fearing the gesture would be too uncouth, nor keep it in his. So he proposes that they leave:

—It's late, Madame. Nicole hasn't gone to bed yet, but it's late.

FOUR

A farewell scene at a railway station in the mountains at the end of the holidays, with numerous handshakes, impatient exclamations, and promises to write and to meet again. The entire guesthouse has come to see Marthe Bonneau off, and they gather around her solitary figure noisily, and she is quiet and vaguely intimidated by their effusions, perhaps a little embarrassed at not being able to be more communicative than she is used to being. She caresses Nicole affectionately and gives precise answers to imprecise questions.

Elsewhere on the platform, Marc is talking animatedly with Renée Rey. Stefan Valeriu notes this detail in passing and wonders for the first time if something has occurred between them which he, with his own preoccupations, has failed to register. But it is a flicker of a thought and he is once again caught up in the atmosphere on the platform, simultaneously sincere and artificial. As the train is about to leave, Madame Bonneau extends her arm out the window to shake his hand and shouts:

—We're waiting for you in Paris! I hope you'll come visit Marc!

Which could be a code, to be understood by them alone. But which might also just mean, I hope you'll come visit Marc.

Funny! concludes Stefan, arriving back at the guest-house an hour later, when, in the garden, he feels very alone and suspended before the remaining four weeks, which look pointless to him now. And with this "Funny!" he decides to draw a line under this amorous interlude which now, in the absence of the woman, seems tiring and far away to him. He looks at the calendar and sees that it's only the middle of August and looks in the guide for a still-unvisited castle in the area. Then he lights his pipe and goes for a wander.

In the evening, after dinner, Stefan finds himself momen-tarily disconcerted, deriving mostly from regret that he's unoccupied at an hour which until yesterday he would have spent with everybody in the common room. Who could re-place Marc at cards or Madame Bonneau in conversation? The windows are open in the common room, the familiar voices within can be heard, blue tobacco smoke drifts in the lamplight. The terrace seems bigger than before, the night deeper, and there is something steady and strong in the far-off reflections on the lake. It's good, very good, to hear the sound of footsteps on the damp earth, to lean against the parapet of the terrace, the entire valley beneath you, not expecting anyone and not wanting anything.

Somebody has approached silently through the grass. It's Renée Rey. He feels her warm breath on his cheek.

—Why are you sad?

He is about to reply sincerely, I'm not sad at all. But this is replaced, almost unintentionally, with:

—What are you asking? You know full well.

Her eyes shine intensely.

Really?

And she falls into his arms, seeking his mouth, her fumbling, inexpert kisses falling where they will. But she has a moment of doubt.

—And Madame Bonneau?

—Madame Bonneau? Don't you understand? It was a game, I had to hide, to mislead you, to prevent anything untoward occurring. But now that you've found out, I will have to leave...

—No, no, no! You have to stay, for me, with me. Oh, if only you could know... And she showers him again with her wild, inexperienced kisses, while from the common room Monsieur Rey calls her to bed, because it's past midnight and the card game has ended.

He is woken, as usual, by the sound of bells: cows ascending a track behind the guesthouse, under his open window. For a few moments he lies with his eyes half-open, lingering in the warmth of semi-slumber, feeling the suggestion between his lashes of the sunlight spilling into the room, mixed with the smell of wet grass and occasional shouts from outside. It was a sudden, triumphant, deep sleep, imbued with happiness, the way the black earth must feel the underground spring that feeds it.

This private victory song bothers him. Stefan Valeriu does not know enough. The fact in hand, last night's little bit of play-acting, should at very most amuse him, but he's delighted with it. That's not good. "I'm an imbecile!" He dresses quickly, slips into his sandals, passes his fingers through his hair a couple of times, throws his bathing suit over his shoulders, and goes downstairs. In the garden, the morning is even more brilliant than he had guessed: the lake sparkles promisingly in the distance.

—Monsieur Valeriu!

The shout is from somewhere above, and Stefan has to scan the front of the building twice to discover Renée at one of the windows, poorly hidden behind curtains.

—Good morning Madame Rey.

—Won't you come up for a minute, to get that book?

—What book?

—The one you lent me . . .

Stefan goes upstairs, to the Reys' bedroom this time. She is waiting for him behind the door, trembling and pale, in her nightgown. Evidently, she's only just risen: the bed is unmade. Stefan carries her to the bed and throws her among the pillows.

—Monsieur Rey?

—Away.

—Nicole?

—Her too.

—How so?

—I love you. If you only knew... if you only knew...

As it turns out, Renée doesn't know how to love. Her first embrace is strikingly awkward: there is no reticence or delay in yielding, only a series of hesitations, more likely from awkwardness than from modesty. But the abruptness of the occurrence, the voices in the garden below, the crumpled bedclothes, the open window—all add up to make their amorous interlude something strange and incongruous.

🙠

Renée has an ugly body. Very delicate hands with weak wrists, thin legs, tanned cheeks, lips burning from a perpetual fever, and rings under her eyes. She has an awkward way of wearing her well-cut dresses that make them look like they don't fit her properly. Only in the cool of evening, when she throws her embroidered silk shawl over her shoulders, enveloping her body in it, does she recover her natural grace. The grace Stefan had noted, with detachment, the first time he saw her. Naked, she becomes younger than she is, and her hips seem all the more blatant because of her long, adolescent thighs.

—Renée, you're the most naked woman in the world.

—You talk nonsense. How can one naked woman be more naked than another naked woman?

—She can. You don't understand. Being naked doesn't mean being undressed. There are naked women and undressed women. You're a naked woman.

Unable to make such a distinction, Renée frowns, only accentuating her sharp, girlish features.

— Do you have any Tunisians in your family, way back?

—A real Tunisian?

—Yes.

—None. Why do you ask?

—I don't know. There's something un-European about you. I'm not sure what it is: the wiry hair, the thin body, your dark skin—and those burning lips.

—No. No Tunisians. We're all like that over there! Maybe it's the sun...

Stefan likes to press his cheek against her skin and to rub it against her body. Her body burns in moments of passion, at other times it is cool and smooth like the leaves of a potted palm. In peaceful moments, released from his arms, Renée lies beside him, tired, her eyes closed, surrounded by an aura of elemental peace. Then, later, she is suddenly, inexplicably seized by shyness at his presence. She covers her face with her hands, squeezes her dark thighs together desperately, retreats into herself, and denies access, absurdly, violently. Until, from exhaustion or a whim, she lets herself go with childish abandon.

After their first hour of love, up in her conjugal bedroom, on a morning nothing had prepared her for, Renée Rey had taken refuge, without explanations, by playing impeccably the role of perfect wife.

Madame Rey, Stefan had whispered at dinner, in passing, I've found a room in the city, in the old town. Tomorrow afternoon at three, we'll have a little walk around the lake and just lose the group. We'll go see the room. Yes?

—No.

He had no time to ask why not, as Monsieur Rey was approaching. Later, when he'd inquired, she spoke stupidly about feeling guilty, about her duties... Which hadn't prevented her, the following afternoon, when everybody else was having coffee in the garden, from coming to his room, falling into his arms and removing her dress with panicked movements and kissing him haphazardly, murmuring from time to time, "if Marcel comes," in a passionate voice, as though it were an exclamation of love rather than of fear, and losing herself in his arms with small, ragged cries while the steps of those passing in the corridor could be heard through the door, which they have left ajar.

Now they are in their room in the old town, where Renée hadn't wanted to come but has come, a white-walled room with metal-frame furniture, open windows, and banal decor amongst which the image of "the outraged husband" would be ridiculous, almost impossible to entertain. Only sometimes, when the subject arises, does Renée cover her face and say with an intonation that is not hers:

—Oh, I'm not deserving of such a husband.

Which is an expression adopted recently, probably from a show at the Comédie-Française, one of the several she saw in Paris, when passing through that city.

❧

Have they been observed? Maybe yes, maybe no. While Renée has been imprudent and emotional, Stefan has been measured and lazy. Is it possible for a young man and a young woman to sleep together in a house full of people with nothing to do, without its being noticed? So far, there's no way to know. Madame Bonneau is sometimes still mentioned, which distracts from other notions. Monsieur Rey plays chess just as well as before and his handshake betrays no suspicion. But on one occasion Nicole has burst into tears, out of the blue, when Stefan asked her something ordinary.

—Why, Nicole? Why?

Monsieur Rey punished her immediately, because "nobody should do things in life for no reason, not even crying."

He's a strange one, thinks Stefan, watching how he takes his time planning his chess moves. Much stranger, in any case, than tiring, scattered, passionate Renée. What plowman's hands! An expression like a lumberjack's! What a stubborn, dull, unworried silence.

There was a light opera performance in town one evening and they'd all attended. They had agreed that morning that it would be formal attire: long dresses and black suits. Meeting at the jetty, awaiting the boat, Marcel Rey had cut a ridiculous figure among all those satin dresses and dinner jackets. He was squeezed into a tight frock coat more suited to a young man's figure, and his felt hat was oversized, as though borrowed. Renée had a little fit of hysteria that she had difficulty suppressing, and Stefan too felt embarrassed by his own elegance, so easily attained and triumphant. Monsieur Rey's right shoulder was higher than the other.

—Impossible to get him to unlearn this bad habit, complained Renée.

—Why should I unlearn it? It's what I'm used to: I carry my gun on that shoulder.

—Gun! exclaims Monsieur Vincent, alarmed.

—Yes, at dawn and dusk, when I inspect the plantations in Djedaida.

Djedaida! How often Stefan has tried to imagine the rough life there of an old colonial family; the grandparents who knew the first colonial war, young cousins who made the journey to Paris long ago and have been melancholy ever since; the festive evenings with everybody gathered at the home of the elder Reys, listening to gramophone recordings, and sleepless nights, awaiting the burning winds blowing in from the desert, a fine dust whitening the tops of the palm trees, silver beneath the moon...

—Oh, why doesn't Marcel want to move to Paris? Imagine how good it would be. I could visit you, we could go out together, drink tea at Berry, on the Champs-Élysées...

—You're right Renée, you don't have any Tunisian blood.

—Why do you say that?

—No reason.

FIVE

O dette Mignon is eighteen. She wears a blue beret, set low on the back of her head, a sports dress with a leather belt, and white sandals with no socks.

Stefan met her one evening on the guesthouse terrace while his friends were playing with a ring and a string and she was looking out at the night falling over the lake.

—Won't you play with us?

—Certainly.

She joined the group and played spiritedly, and sang along with everybody when the time came:

Il court, il court le furet,
Le furet du bois joli . . .

The ring was slipped secretly from hand to hand and the player in the middle had to guess who had it, requiring the others to pass it quickly on, or to feign doing so. Renée Rey, beside Stefan, had license to squeeze his hand hard, which caused him to let himself be caught several times so that he could leave the group and, later, sit beside Odette, who was playing seriously, in good faith, sportingly, with no more hand-squeezing than the game required.

~

It rained all day and it was evening, at dinnertime, at seven, before it brightened a little on the right side of the lake. From the dining room windows the distant mountains were violently illuminated by the setting sun.

—A rainbow! somebody cried and everybody jumped up from the table, Monsieur Vincent with his napkin tucked into his collar, Renée noisy, the children amazed, all running out to the terrace, where the wonder could be better observed: an immense rainbow, spanning the valley and coloring the lake an otherworldly blue. Only Stefan Valeriu remained in his place, eating calmly, and in another corner of the dining room sat Odette Mignon, equally unmoved.

—Aren't you curious to see the rainbow? he asked.

—No.

—But it must be beautiful.

—Very. But rather trivial.

She's in form, thinks Stefan, giving her a nod of approval, with the professional admiration with which a soccer forward would salute a team member who had scored a nice goal.

~

If he could have managed it without it seeming obvious, Stefan would not have sat beside Renée Rey on the bus. But it was unavoidable. It's a tour bus, with rows of benches, each seating three people. Renée is on Stefan's right and Odette is on his left. Monsieur Rey rides right up in front, beside the driver, with a guidebook in his hand, imparting geographical-historical information.

—Attention, Le Col de la Caussade! Attention, Pont du Query! Altitude, 1,816 meters. No, beg your pardon, 1,716...

The driver sometimes stops and turns off the motor so that he can take a photograph or shoot a few meters of film. As the sun has not yet risen and it's very cold, they've pulled blankets over themselves, which allows Renée to take Stefan's hand and grip it with feeling, while to his left Odette gesticulates in the cold air of five a.m., pointing toward the distance at a poplar or a peak or a fishing net in a lake.

Stefan is deeply, inordinately depressed at having his hand imprisoned and thinks he would be instantly happy had he the courage to tear it free. He feels the woman's heavy, soft, still-sleepy arm, and this feeling of being tucked away cozily somewhere strikes him as obscene on this pure new morning, vibrating with light and sound.

—You don't love me anymore.

—Oh, I do, I do. (And if he didn't know it was useless, he'd tell her that now that's not the issue, and that she's stupidly confusing things; things which bear no relation one to the other.)

They stopped, toward lunch, at a Carthusian monastery very near to Grenoble and made the obligatory visit through the cells, library, and chapel, led by a guide who made perfunctory announcements. Here Saint Bruno maintained his vow of silence for three years, here's a stained glass window from the thirteenth century, here the pope slept one night when he was crossing the mountains toward Avignon...

Renée acted very interested in this information and tarried behind the group, hanging on Stefan's arm, asking him for further explanations, in order to steal a kiss from him behind a door or around a corner in a hallway. In a cell, Stefan caught her caressing the bed boards and thought, unkindly, that she was thinking how uncomfortable it would have been to make love there.

Only on arriving in Grenoble was he able to shake off the group. He enjoyed the unexpected freedom of exploring the streets of an unfamiliar city, where nobody knew him and he knew nobody. He turned his head to look at his reflection in the windows of the shops he passed and the tall figure he saw there was like that of an old friend.

In a bookshop he browsed through new books and magazines that had all appeared in the previous two months, before his disappearance from the world. Greedy for information, he plied the salesman with questions. The salesman was taken aback by this client, who bought nothing and wanted to know everything.

He almost didn't notice Odette Mignon, who had also come into the shop and was surprised to see him there.

—If you'll allow me the pleasure, let me choose a book for you. As a gift. Look, this one, for example!

Handing her the book, he felt how the gesture of giving something had the effect of immediately erasing the memory of that awful morning and redeeming it.

🔖

Monsieur Rey has pinned up a notice in the dining room, in handwritten capital letters:

THIS EVENING
a unique, great cinematographic event
on the guesthouse terrace
In tonight's program
some very special short films

Indeed, all the films sent to be developed in Paris have come back—all the excursions, the long walks around the lake, several afternoons on the terrace... So many scenes they had forgotten and believed lost, and yet they continue to exist in that wooden box, delivered by post. They all feel a kind of stage fright, as before a premiere, and pass the time before evening in nervous, impatient discussion.

—It's going to be wonderful! As long as it's in focus. You remember that picnic tea we had, when we did the walk around the lake? I'd love to see how it turned out. It'll be wonderful, wonderful...

The newer guests, who were not part of the earlier group, also get caught up in the general excitement, as everyone is invited to the showing—a kind of regional gala premiere. As it gets dark, Monsieur Rey sets up a screen and the projector, and Renée, acting as hostess, shows people to their seats, keeping Stefan beside her and placing Odette, as it happens, at the far corner, beside Monsieur Vincent and Nicole.

The first meters of film are greeted noisily, with each person recognizing themselves on the screen with an exclamation—the ladies with short enthusiastic cries (Oh! Goodness! Look! No! Not that!), the men with the hint of a vain smile or—in the case of Monsieur Vincent—with explosive laughter, as though to say, each time he reappeared on-screen, "Oh, that's a good one."

Stefan finds it hard to identify with his unreal, somehow impossible, image on the screen. He finds it unnatural that while sitting still, there in the garden, on a white wicker chair, somebody else, who also happens to be he, is walking about, free—freer, it would seem, than his true self—as though having escaped from under his control forever.

Look, Marthe Bonneau, in a boat, and there goes Marc, running along a pathway after who knows whom, and there's Marthe again, regal, cinematic, and eternally beautiful.

The scene changes again: the walk at Lovagny. ("Remember, Stefan? It was the day after we met.") But why is the Renée on the screen always holding his arm? Why is she now leaning on his shoulder? Wherefore that tender air, which he does not recall? No. It's impossible. It wasn't like that. It couldn't have been. They were strangers. He addressed her respectfully. She responded coldly. Everything on the screen is unrecognizable; everything is altered to become livelier, warmer, and more intimate.

The longer the film goes on—more scenes, more walks—the more daring the gestures of the woman on the screen become. An air of complicity gathers around the pair of them and though the jerky images show nothing flagrant, there are relentless hints of intimacy. There is something adulterous in all these pictures, though it would be hard to say exactly what. Perhaps something distracted in Renée's eyes, perhaps the constant absence of her husband, who never appears in frame, being busy behind the camera. Stefan feels that the people around him are laughing less, or perhaps louder. In any case, differently, in embarrassment, as though everybody has figured it out.

—Marcel, that's enough. We can continue tomorrow evening. It's late.

—But why, Renée, my dear? It's only eleven, and everyone's having fun. Isn't that right, ladies and gentlemen?

Anyway, I haven't even shown half of it. Look, this scene for example. Remember? In the old town, when I stayed behind to buy stamps...

—Marcel, please...

—...and you'd gone ahead with Monsieur Valeriu. Look, I keep filming until you're both around the corner.

Does he know? If so, why is he so at ease? If not, why does he insist on explaining every scene and providing pathetic explanations that nobody needs? Stefan Valeriu no longer understands anything. He's afraid to look up, and sometimes, feeling a pair of eyes on him, twitches uncomfortably. Only Odette Mignon meets his eyes clearly and guilelessly, as always. She at least will not suspect anything.

How much simpler things are the next morning on the lake, when Stefan stretches out on the bottom of the boat, drifting, oars floating. How the troubles above, in the pension, its little dramas and tiresome heroines, fade into the distance and vanish! Then Odette Mignon, his swimming and rowing partner, appears at the bow, bare-limbed, tanned, and comradely, like a new Marc Bonneau, interrupting the blue expanse between the mountains that Stefan has been studying.

—Has Madame Rey been your lover for long?

—My lover?

—Yes. I'm asking if you've been sleeping together for long now.

The bluntness of the question does not permit a response. In any case, Odette doesn't seem to expect one.

—Oh, in that respect Monsieur Rey's documentaries certainly do some documenting. They were wonderful. If you hadn't been so grumpy yesterday we could have got together and have talked all about it.

—They were truly uncomfortable moments, I can assure you.

—I know. But I suspected something was up because, personally, I had nothing else to do to amuse myself. But I think you took it far too seriously, and still do. Nobody noticed.

—You think?

—I'm sure. There were only hints on the screen. Nothing definite. No kisses, for example. Nothing so incontrovertible. And none of our friends up there are capable of reading the signs. Rainbow-gawkers...

—And Monsieur Rey?

—A mystery. He intrigues me so much, that if I thought he'd tell me I'd run to him now, in my dripping bathing suit, hair all over the place, and ask him. Either he's one tough guy or he's a fool.

—How old are you, Odette?

—You already asked. Eighteen.

—You're intelligent and know a few things.

—I'm a virgin. That helps me be intelligent. Also, I've lived on my own a lot. My parents divorced when I was twelve. Mama is still young. Daddy's rich and ambitious. Both of them have continued to love and to keep going, each in their own way. Both have shared confidences with me, as you would with a friend. As well they might. I wasn't a little girl any more. I'd grown up fast and wasn't bored by anything. I've learned all I know from them: I think I've managed to give them useful advice sometimes. To Daddy, when he needed a new tie, at the beginning of an affair, Mama, when she felt life was over after some fool left her.

—You're a boy, Odette.

—As you wish...

—A boy in a blue beret, a white dress, and wooden sandals, with blond hair, little fists, and dark-blue eyes. If you were a bit uglier, I could have given you a pair of boots, taught you to smoke a pipe, and we would have headed for the mountains, to sleep in cabins, each on hard boards, far from love and swooning and psychological complications.

❧

Renée Rey is sick. Her blinds have been down all day. She was absent at lunch, but Monsieur Rey, who came down with Nicole, lunched somberly and with a good appetite.

—He's a brute, said somebody, a lady in the guesthouse.

He's a simple man, thought Odette.

The doctor came downstairs. Renée had not wanted to see him, but her husband was firm.

—I have to know what's wrong with her.

"Nothing wrong with her," was the doctor's reply as he left and this almost made Monsieur Rey lose his temper. He settled for pacing the garden gloomily.

—Well, as long as there's nothing wrong with her, you needn't be upset, observed Odette innocently.

—There's nothing wrong with her but she's pale, nothing wrong with her but she doesn't eat, nothing wrong with her but she faints. For a farmer's wife, this illness is too subtle. Over there, we're either healthy or we're stretched out, we stay on our feet or fall over. We're properly hale and hearty or else properly sick.

Shortly after the doctor had left, while Odette was listening to Monsieur Rey's explanations in the garden, a servant sought Stefan Valeriu.

—Madame Rey insists you come upstairs.

He found her naked, stretched diagonally across the double bed, very pale but with her eyes shining feverishly. The light of dusk, reduced further by the heavy drapes, fully drawn, increased her pallor and cast heavy shadows across the pillows.

—Are you sick?

—No, I'm in love with you.

—My dear Renée, that's very nice, but is this really the time to tell me? When your husband, alarmed, might come up here at any moment? When the entire guesthouse has its eyes glued to the patient's windows?

—You'll never understand. Touch me with your hand, see how I'm burning up. Kiss me, and see how I've waited for you. My man...my love...you're mine!

It was as though her body were begging him, revealing its most secret, private places, down to the deep, dumb roots of life. He felt that if he got any closer to her it would not be her burning lips or her gleaming Arab thighs he would feel, but her aorta pulsing with too much blood, veins, and a heart like a wound.

He hesitated for a second and, in the tumult drawing him toward the woman in front of him, the thought that something definitive was being decided made something snap. He turned about, opened the door, slammed it behind him, and ran down the stairs—free.

A telegram was waiting for Odette in the dining room, on her table, at dinnertime. She opened it and read it without hurry.

—It's from Daddy. He's coming by in his automobile the day after tomorrow, in the morning, to pick me up. We're going to Antibes.

—Were you expecting him?

—No, but he likes to be a bit dramatic. He knows I like it too.

❧

Odette is in her room, having gone up after the evening meal to write some letters and put a few things in order.

—I want to be free all day tomorrow so it's better if I get ready tonight. Daddy doesn't like to be kept waiting. Good night.

—Good night. I'll be here. But if you like, later, on my way to bed, I'll knock on your door for a little chat.

—Please do.

It's been a long time since Stefan has been on his own on the terrace at night. Perhaps not since Madame Bonneau's departure, before this long love affair had begun.

How good it must have been then, he thinks, trying to remember, watching a firefly light up in the dark, like the pulse of a heart. He would happily forget everything that has happened since and to remember only this vast night, and the point of light created by this firefly.

Pity it isn't raining. He would stay out in it, bareheaded and with nothing around his neck, sleeves rolled up, leaning against a tree trunk, letting the water stream through his hair, down his forehead and cheeks, until he felt, together with the grass around him, part of the slumbering, insensible earth, free forever from guilt and remorse, free from the obsession behind those dimly lighted windows up there, where a passionate woman was in the grip of excessive love.

But it isn't raining and it isn't going to rain, and the night is unbearably beautiful with this dramatic lake, its waters reflecting the full moon and the stars and the silver mountains. Never rains when you need it, Stefan thinks acidly, and turns to go to bed, glad that at least he'll tarry a quarter of an hour in Odette's room before retiring, to talk about various nothings. But there is no response when he knocks on the door.

—Odette!

Her light is on, however, and he can clearly hear her tense breathing on the other side of the door.

—Odette, what's this nonsense? Why won't you answer?

—Oh, it's you. Good evening.

—Good evening. I came to talk with you a bit.

—Oh, it's late now. I hope you don't mind, but I'm sleepy.

—I don't mind at all. Just open up so I can shake your hand.

Stefan waits for a few seconds, not sure whether he is amused or annoyed by what is happening.

—Listen, Odette. I'm serious: if there's some reason you can't see me, tell me what it is and I'll go. But if there's no reason, open up for a moment. I'll just say good night and go to bed. I'm tired too.

—There's absolutely nothing wrong, but I can't open the door.

—Why?

—Just because.

—I'll have you know I'm not leaving here until either you give me a proper explanation or you open up.

She doesn't reply and Stefan visualizes her on the other side of the door, annoyed, balling her fists, lower lip drawn downward, with the nervous smile she has during a quarrel whenever she feels helpless.

—I'm going to wait here, you know. I've lit my pipe and I'm leaning against the wall, comfortably, my hand in my pocket, waiting. Until one, until two, until morning...

Odette has put out the light. Probably she has got into bed and is listening carefully to hear if he has gone. Sometimes, quietly, pleadingly, like an annoyed child, fighting against sleep, she whispers something.

—Stefan, go to bed. Stefan, it's late. Stefan, you'll be tired tomorrow...

It's his turn not to reply, frowning and surly, determined to stay, but knowing the door is not going to open that night.

꧁

Stefan Valeriu went away at daybreak and didn't return until late in the evening, when dinner was over. He rambled through several local villages, smoked an enormous amount, and had very serious conversations with peasants he met about the crops and the weather.

Maybe it isn't nice to run off, he thought several times on his journey, but Renée Rey's mysteriously shut windows encouraged him, even from afar, to keep going.

—It's better this way. Much better.

As for Odette, it would be a good thing to tweak her ear as though she were a cheeky kid and let her know what he thought of the previous evening's prank, which he had not enjoyed one bit.

Back at the guesthouse, he is very glad it's late, with the dining room deserted and everybody gone to bed. The lights are low in the Reys' window, Odette Mignon's is dark.

—All the better!

Still, he should bid her a good journey. She'll be gone tomorrow before daybreak and he'll certainly never see her again.

—She was sweet sometimes...

And, going upstairs to his room, he smiles when he realizes that with those words he has reached the end of the story with that beautiful, slightly screwy, blue-eyed girl. He's bone-tired, and with each step upward he feels closer to the imminent bliss of removing his boots, stretching out his naked arms and falling onto his cool bedsheets. Seven more steps, two more, finally there. His hand falls heavily on the door handle, he opens the door and enters his room—with the hazy sensuality of a returning wanderer—and turns on the lamp.

—Good evening, Odette.

Why wasn't he startled? It would have been natural and reasonable to react like that. A little jolt at least, finding her there in his room, in his bed, at such an hour, naked, calm, and familiar. But instead of amazement and noisy exclamations, all he can find to say is "Good evening, Odette."

—Good evening, Stefan.

He goes to her and kisses both her cheeks, caresses her rounded knees and then takes off his rucksack.

—You know, I'm whacked. I've walked an incredible distance today. Have you been waiting long for me?

—A couple of hours.

—Didn't it drag?

—No. I turned off the light, undressed, and got into bed. The view from here is lovely, toward the forest.

He continued to undress, without haste or excitement.

—Anything new in the guesthouse?

—Nothing. Madame Rey didn't come down today either. Monsieur Rey asked after you. I said my farewells to all of them in the evening and went to get my bags ready. I only left out my travel dress and look, you've gone and sat on it.

—Sorry. Will I turn the light out?

He's standing naked in front of the bed, relaxed and unashamed, as though they are friends who have known each other for a long time.

—Yes, do.

They embrace in silence, and his arms envelop her. He explores her from the top of her head to her ankles, glad that her robust yet fine body is neither trembling nor impatient. He feels her calm breasts, hears the steady beating of her heart, her peaceful breathing. The girl's thighs open like wings, yieldingly but deliberately.

Her body is attentive and receptive, following his suggestions trustingly, responsive like the keys of a piano to his touch. They don't need to struggle to find each other in the dark, don't lose each other, don't speak: the harmony is that of two stalks, growing, entwined. And Odette's clear, sharp cry—a single cry—of pain, of triumph, of freedom, doesn't frighten either of them, and flies through the open window and is lost in the woods, where it wakes a squirrel perhaps, or blends with the distant and equally free call of a wildcat.

—Are you crying, Odette?

She isn't. She is warmer than before, and her hurt body presses more closely to his, still firm and sure, but her shoulders are heavier and her defeated hands lie on the pillows.

—Are you sleepy, Odette?

No, she isn't. She has never been more awake, never been less confused, more aware of what is happening. Look, this is your hand, this is my knee, these are your rough lips, this is my ear that you're kissing without its sending a shiver through me, that's your too-broad shoulder blade, and these are my wrists and over there, look, the first rays of daybreak...Soon, from Serrier, the sound of an approaching automobile will be heard. You have to go, the car down there is beeping its horn, calling you from the roadway.

Why doesn't she cry, why doesn't she ask him to make her stay, why doesn't she cling to him more desperately, why does she stay so close beside him and why does she love him as though it's forever and not just for an hour?

Odette is standing in the doorway in the same white dress and blue beret she wore that first day, about to leave, suitcase in hand.

—Goodbye, Stefan.

She stands in the threshold.

—Odette?

—Yes?

—Tell me now. Why wouldn't you open the door the other evening?

She thinks for a moment.

—I don't know, Stefan. I really don't!

SIX

September has arrived, lovely in its weakening light. There are fewer boats on the lake, their sails have been furled, and the white passenger ferries make fewer trips. A notice on the jetty announces that the 8:27 service will no longer run. With each passing day, more shutters close over the windows of the guesthouse: people are leaving. Will that window, today laughing in the sun, its white curtains fluttering, be open again tomorrow? And the one beside it? And the one above? One by one they close, like lights going out.

For the past several days, Renée Rey has left her room. After lunch, at around two o'clock, she takes a walk either alone or with Monsieur Rey. She takes his arm and they walk in silence. Sometimes they stop to pet the guesthouse's huge, shaggy sheepdog. Madame Rey is paler than before and looks taller, and when anybody comes across her she smiles like a convalescent. She has spoken a few inconsequential words with Stefan, with no more sadness than when speaking to the others.

—It's so lovely outside and it was horrible up there in my room. I missed you all, and the sun.

It seems they will be gone in a day or two. They've written ahead to Marseille to inquire about the weather, as Renée needs a calm crossing. In the evening she reclines on a chaise longue while Monsieur Rey and Stefan play chess. Just as in the first days. When it is completely dark, the lights of the train station far beyond the lake can be seen, and the Paris train at midnight, like a thick, articulated, phosphorescent snake. They pause in the middle of their game and watch it until it disappears.

—We have a tough life, says Monsieur Rey, breaking the silence. I don't regret it and wouldn't change it. But it is tough. I'm sure Renée has tears in her eyes, watching that same train, which she won't be taking again for who knows how many years. Maybe never. That doesn't scare me, but, you see, there's something in me, a kind of affliction, that gives me pause. I know it'll pass. It will pass for her too. Work takes care of all that. The sun, the plantations, the desert, the breeze at night, the Arabs... But you have to understand how different things are here, how appealing it is and how a woman in particular would find it all irresistible...

He forgets about the game and speaks quietly, the furrow between his eyebrows deeper than usual. Then he suddenly stands up.

—I'm going up to pack. We're leaving tomorrow. Stay with Renée until I come back.

Stefan goes to the terrace, where Madame Rey's shawl is dimly visible in the darkness.

—Monsieur Rey went upstairs. He asked me to keep you company. May I?

—Of course.

—It seems you're leaving tomorrow.

—I didn't know, but all the better.

He sits on the grass and for a long time doesn't speak, listening to the breathing of the woman next to him. He sees a firefly, captures it, holds it in his fist to better see how the little creature extinguishes the little lamp in its head, but she asks him to put it in her hair and he does this. In the dark, the glowing spark looks like an enormous hair clasp, just bright enough to backlight her head with a faint aura.

Everything seems completely peaceful and then Renée bursts into tears. Good, friendly tears which Stefan helps along, caressing her hands, receiving the weeping with equanimity, as he would the rain.

—Will you be staying on long, Stefan?

—I don't really know. I'm waiting for news from back in my country. Perhaps a week. Maybe longer.

—You don't mind me crying?

—Why should I, Renée? It's nighttime. Nobody can see. And somebody needs to cry for us all.

꧁

Nothing else happens and the days pass pointlessly, leaving behind them the air of an unlived-in, unfurnished house, its rooms resounding with the footfalls of a solitary visitor. The morning light is raw, like egg white, and the light of evening as warm as the porcelain bowl of a kerosene lamp. A photograph has arrived from the Rey family, sent from Marseille on the eve of their departure, along with their friendly regards. Stefan has placed it in the frame of his mirror and he expects he will leave it there when he departs. A letter has arrived for Odette Mignon and the owner of the guesthouse has given it to Stefan, as she has no forwarding address. Stefan doesn't know it either. It's strange that Odette didn't offer such information, stranger still that Stefan didn't ask for it. Several forgotten items have been found in her room: a piece of embroidery, a book, a scarf, and three or four amateur photographs. They show a flighty-looking Odette, her skirts flapping in the wind, her blue beret askew, her hands aloft to catch some imaginary ball. "She passed by like a girl you'd meet on a tram," says Stefan, looking out the window, toward the empty lake, across which a single sailboat hastens, like a frightened bird. Near the jetty, several seagulls swoop low and skim the water with their bellies, then rise again, disoriented. The glum footfalls of the lame chambermaid, Anetta, can be heard as she makes her rounds of the rooms before dark, to check that all is in order.

—Madame Bernard wonders if you'd like a fire. It's got cold and it's supposed to rain tonight.

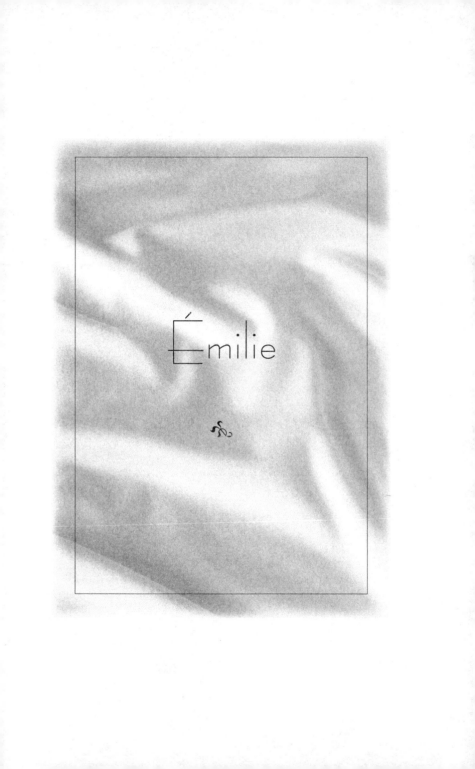

Émilie

ONE

Why Émilie Vignou remained a virgin until the evening she met Irimia C. Irimia, I couldn't tell you. Laziness or a lack of imagination. Everything should have worked against such enduring chastity; the example of her friends, the loose ways that prevailed in her neighborhood, and an impoverished, joyless life. She was a girl of twenty when I met her first. Hefty, slow-witted, and sluggish. I wondered sometimes what she'd been like before, as a child, but despite my best efforts I couldn't imagine it.

In short, she was a docile creature and, ugly as she was, she had an air of resignation about her sometimes that I liked. Still today, after all this time, I can't think of her without a certain sad sympathy, and the thought of writing her story consoles me a little for losing her. It's a feeling she wouldn't have understood. She would have blinked her little eyes and, feeling that it had something to do with her after all, she would have smiled—her usual smile, vague and unlovely.

I remember the evening I met her. It was in January, in a period during which I was trying to salve a secret melancholy that had endured for some three months, since a holiday I'd spent by an Alpine lake, where I'd gone for the summer to rest up after some exhausting final medical exams. I'd returned from there with the memory, which still troubles me sometimes, of a blond woman who'd loved me for no reason and disappeared in the same way, without explanations. I was trying to get over it and to get back on track with my minor successes as a young man, waiting that day for Mado, the lively girl I'd got talking to a long time previously in a Métro station and who was still hesitating in the face of my amorous advances. (I later learned that in her neighborhood any serious liaison required preparatory meetings. It was a matter of good form and I should have observed the proprieties.) It was raining that Sunday and we searched in vain for a place to go. Completely full at the *bal-musette*, completely sold out at the cinema. We plodded about in the rain, stopping occasionally to shelter under a balcony. I, bored of this too-virtuous affair, Mado trembling from cold at my arm. Finally, despairing of finding any place to go and with the rain getting heavier, she made a decision.

—Come on, let's go to Émilie's place!

I understood she was about to surrender her virtue and didn't ask for explanations. That was when I first entered Émilie Vignou's room. It was a garret in a dirty, lopsided house that leaned over the tracks somewhere near the Porte de Saint-Ouen. From up there you'd hear the regular whistling of the trains on the ring line and, when you opened the window, a dull rumble of the suburban street. I didn't get a good look at the woman who lived there. All I registered when we entered was a shadow of a woman in a dim corner, getting up. Mado gave her a friendly pat on the shoulder as she slipped away without a word.

Here's not the place to talk about Mado and it wouldn't be interesting. Suffice to say that she was an affectionate, worthy partner. She had two hours of wandering in the rain to make up for and make up for them she did. She was naked and passionate. It was only when silence had descended after her first amorous transports that I noticed, with horror, the shape of the woman whom I'd believed to have left the room hunched there on a low stool in a corner in the dark. I can't stand that sort of sleaziness and was about to complain roughly to the woman next to me, who was sinking into the pillows like a satisfied filly, but— understanding my frown—she said casually:

—Oh, it's nothing. That's Émilie.

She said this with vast indifference, as though remarking a cat or a piece of furniture. On the other hand, the shadow in the corner didn't show any sign of life, so even I, who found intolerable the idea of sleeping with a woman while another is present, paid her no further mind and responded appropriately to my young companion's enthusiasms.

I met Émilie Vignou a few times after that. Mado sent her to me on various errands, and the poor girl walked for kilometers just to deliver love letters. I can still see her in the lobby of the Trousseau hospital, where I was doing my internship at the time, with her faded velvet hat and long overcoat of nondescript color, fidgeting with the envelope she'd brought and not knowing how to hand it over. Every movement she had to make was torture for her and I don't think I'll ever forget the excruciating time I spent with her in the duty room, where I'd invited her to eat with me, thinking she'd enjoy it. She didn't know what to do with her hands, how to hide them, and beneath the surface she suffered greatly. I think her entire life had been poisoned by that pair of hands, and her instinctive sense of their uselessness. It was as though they didn't belong to her; they were too unwieldy and heavy. Just looking at them, I had a sense that they weighed her down. They were a permanent burden, and I wonder if Émilie would have died in the end from exhaustion if—as we shall see—an accident had not killed her first.

Whenever Émilie was troubled or unhappy, or enraged, I would observe her running her hands down her dress, as though looking for a place to hide them or to grip onto something. Many times since, I've thought Émilie's life would have been much simpler had her dress just had pockets.

There was something painful in her stiffness that prevented me from laughing. Her body only bent because of her uneven gait. Émilie was not what you could properly call a cripple; she wasn't an invalid. But she had a habit of leaning more on her left foot; something she'd picked up from her job. She worked in the basement of a big department store, in the packing section, and spent her whole day working a pedal that unspooled string for tying up packages. She'd been doing this eight hours a day, every day, for years. Her left foot had learned the steady rhythm of the pedal and she couldn't unlearn it.

But I've nothing more to say about how Émilie looked. I've said she was ugly and that will suffice. Since, in any case, you wouldn't understand what sweetness her ugliness held. I was fond of her, and all her friends, who tortured her with all kinds of awful errands, and will never forget the docile expression on her face.

She was as quiet as a dormouse. She stole by you without a word when she felt superfluous, without speaking, without asking anything. When we brought her with us on the town, to dances in our quarter, she stayed apart to guard the coats. And when one of her friends needed someone to accompany her on an amorous encounter, Émilie would always be present for the most sensual scenes. I don't know if her friends did this deliberately, to exasperate her. I don't know if Émilie suffered as a result of these shows. I just know that she sat there, unmoved, watching what was going on calmly and dully.

How Émilie Vignou could remain a virgin while living such a life is hard to understand. Prudish she was not.

Social conventions were not a factor, as in her world to be a virgin after the age of fifteen was scandalous.

I think making love was more a physical difficulty than a moral one for her. At the risk of using an ambiguous expression, I'd say that for her love had become a problem of balance. What must have seemed impossible for her about love was losing her center of gravity. Being a vertical creature and then assuming a horizontal position—that's what I believed tortured her sensual dreams, if she ever had any. I think the whole mystery of love was summed up for her in this fact, and she couldn't get her head around it.

I'd beg the reader's pardon for these vulgar details but, to tell the truth, I don't much care about the reader and I care very much about Émilie Vignou. I'm recounting her life in the first place because I want to keep her image alive, here on earth, and second because I want to understand a little about the heart of a girl whom I perhaps passed heedlessly by at another time. So I'm saying that only physical rigidity stopped Émilie from being a good lover. Who can tell what simple love might otherwise have shone from her ashen eyes? But how can you love somebody with a body like hers, made of a single, inflexible piece? I think of Mado's long thighs, I think of how her little body twisted that evening as she writhed in my arms, and try to imagine Émilie doing the same. No, no. The image strikes me as grotesque. If each of us were created with our true vocation in mind, Émilie Vignou would have been a rough-hewn table leg.

It was the only role she could have played well and easily. Who knows? Perhaps she was anatomically unique and had a special form of grace that I was blind to. Her body was bound together in secret ways. When she raised a shoulder, she had to bend a knee. As though any movement threw her off balance and had to be compensated for by another movement. Émilie couldn't move a finger without moving her entire hand from the wrist. A fellow intern who saw Émilie several times in the hospital yard when Mado had sent her looking for me, once told me jokingly:

—Strange! This girl seems to move as if she had multiple sprains.

That was it. Whenever Émilie moved, I expected to hear the crack of bones breaking. I'm afraid all these details, set out like this, paint a repulsive picture of Émilie. That would be a shame. There was something so gentle and homely about her, like a household object that's no longer any use, yet you don't throw it away because you're fond of it for some reason. I liked Émilie exactly as she was and even though I never told her I think she understood and that she felt a certain gratitude toward me. Perhaps it was one of the few pleasant things in her life; at the age of twenty, she had nothing to look forward to. She seemed destined to go on as she was for her remaining days, and that's certainly what would have happened had chance not brought Irimia C. Irimia before her.

TWO

can't say I was pleased that Fourteenth of July, when I crossed paths with him at the Pont Saint-Michel. I was leafing through a pile of old magazines at a secondhand bookseller's on the quays and it's not a pleasure I like to share with anyone.

—Oh, Valerie! (We'd known each other long but he made no great effort to pronounce my name—Stefan Valeriu—correctly, as he found it an odd sort of name, while "Valerie" sounded more familiar and local.) Irimia planted himself before me and I could tell by his silence that he wasn't going to leave there alone.

—What are you up to, Irimia?

—Oh, just looking around...

Indeed, he was just looking. He watched the water flowing under the bridge and his big eyes didn't even blink. I took him with me for a stroll along the quays. He told me in that familiar, rough voice of his that he'd got his law degree in June in Bucharest and was thinking of doing a doctorate in Paris. He'd obtained a grant to do this and had arrived two weeks before from our country. He wanted to learn French by autumn, when the academic year began.

—Because, you know, right now, it's no good. No good at all.

He spoke haltingly, in fragments of sentences, and it was a victory any time he managed to fully articulate an idea. I remembered how he suffered at school, when he had to recite the lesson in front of the history teacher; it was as though each word were a brick he had to dislodge with a hammer from an edifice that in his mind at least was well constructed and handsome.

Poor Irimia! What ridiculous circumstances had taken this peasant from Ialomita and thrust him among that class of society fellows in Lazar high school? What error of judgment had diverted him from his destiny as a plowman and set him struggling with things he had no aptitude for? We'd been classmates since the start of high school and I'd had time to get to know him: he was so tall and heavy, his shoulders and feet so huge, that he barely fitted at his desk. Time and time again, after he'd recited the lesson he'd learned off so laboriously the previous evening, the teacher would send him back to his seat by saying, in a bored voice: "Irimia C. Irimia, return to your place!" I imagined Irimia one day walking quietly to where his coat was hanging and taking it from the hook and saying, in his usual slow voice, that he was not in his proper place. But no. He didn't come from a race of rebels. He went tamely back to his desk, crossed his arms over his chest, and sat there quietly and watched and listened, hulking and ungraceful in that cramped space. I sensed that behind Irimia's obedience lay the melancholy of a domesticated animal that watched and waited, yet retained in the deepest recesses of its being the appetite for another life, and felt the call of other horizons. Maybe I was mistaken. But I didn't know how else to interpret that big fellow's docile smile; an awkward smile that seemed to be permanently begging forgiveness for some mistake.

I have two particular memories of Irimia, neither of which has anything to do with the other, but they have remained distinct in my mind. One was in the schoolyard. An old peasant with an overcoat and saddlebags was at the gate, looking through the bars, not daring to enter. I asked him whom he was looking for.

—Well, my sister's boy.

—What's the boy's name?

—Well, he goes by the name of Irimia.

I sought out Irimia C. Irimia, though there must have been other boys in that high school of the same name. I don't know what told me it was he whom the old man at the gate was looking for. Perhaps his blue eyes, tinged with apprehension, which were the same as the boy's. He was the one, as it turned out. He approached the gate unhurriedly, unsurprised, took off his cap (in the same time-honored way that his ancestors for centuries had doffed their caps), bowed and kissed the old man's chapped, brown, bony hand. I didn't laugh. There was something awesome in the way this giant bowed to the old man, arching over him. I, who have lived in a world of false traditions and false laws, sensed myself in the presence of something eternal, and my schoolmate, Irimia C. Irimia, was enacting it there, in front of me, in the street, by kissing the old man's hand.

My second memory of Irimia is totally unremarkable, and I wonder if it's even worth mentioning. It was also at school, during a lesson on French literature. The teacher had asked him to read aloud a passage from Racine. It's odd that even though it was just a fragment, I still remember today that it was from scene four of the first act of *Andromaque*:

Songez-y bien: il faut désormais que mon coeur,
S'il n'aime avec transport, haïsse avec fureur.

It's hard to describe how Irimia's mouth transformed those verses. A dialect of Bulgarian, crushed between his teeth, without vowels, battered and bruised and abused between two pieces of flint. It caused an uproar of amusement in class and I participated. Steadfast, brows furrowed, his face tensed and his jaws clenching like those of some carnivore, and his immense hands clamped on the covers of the book, Irimia C. Irimia continued reading from Racine. A classmate, whom I personally couldn't stand, though he has since become well-known and writes weekly columns in a reactionary newspaper, an able, intellectual lad (I acknowledge all this so that it's not imagined that I'm somehow jealous, I who haven't made my mark and don't write literature)—this classmate whispered in my ear, then, looking at Irimia:

—He's a primitive.

No, Irimia was just a peasant from Baragan. There, in our midst, reading French verses, I found him ridiculous. But I imagined him at seven o'clock on a July evening, returning to his village barefoot after a long day's work along the edge of a field of grain, in the light of the setting sun, and I told myself that none among us, not one of us smart boys would, in any aspect of our clever lives, have even a scrap of the simple greatness that Irimia possessed in such a moment.

I don't hear what's labeled the "call of the soil" and find pastoral literature risible. But I do enjoy seeing a beautiful creature flourishing in its proper environment. And I sometimes find myself suffering at the sight of a huge circus dog bedecked with ribbons and bells, yoked to its job, knowing that it was made to face wolves on a mountaintop, before God and the pale stars. That, I think, is why I treated Irimia decently, and if I happened to laugh at him a few times, it was from laziness or cowardice: I found it hard not to follow the crowd. Regardless of that, I felt a sincere and straightforward friendliness toward him.

THREE

till, I was bored on that Fourteenth of July. It was a beautiful evening, little flags fluttered from the white boats all along the Seine as they headed toward Vincennes, and Notre-Dame was turning blue on my left, in the dusk. Irimia had finished telling me his story and I'd asked him all the questions I could about it, and we were walking on in silence, stopping from time to time. I would have liked to lose myself alone in that festive crowd, to wander freely and to stop where I wanted. But to no avail. Irimia's boots pounded the ground beside me.

I started to feel worried. I had a date with Mado in the Latin Quarter at ten that evening and saw no way of shaking Irimia off. I say this here not to justify myself, but to clarify the role I unwittingly played in the unfortunate events which were to unfold: I did all I could to get rid of him. I like jokes, but those of my friends who maintain that I set up the farce that was the coupling of Irimia C. Irimia and Émilie Vignou are lying. Perhaps I'm guilty in some respects, and I'll get to that. But on this one count, my conscience is clear: it wasn't I who brought Irimia to the Café D'Harcourt. He stuck to me and came along, against my wishes. I also didn't know that Émilie was coming that evening. I found her there, at the corner of a table, and hardly registered her before Mado was hanging from my neck, kissing me with all the ardor of a little mistress. We hadn't seen each other for several days and she found such holidays from love hard to bear. Also, it was the Fourteenth of July and Mado was a thoroughgoing republican. She grabbed my arm and pulled me out into the middle of the street, where people were dancing in celebration of the fall of the Bastille. I celebrated too. A number of my friends were there, each with his girlfriend, and we partied madly, dancing in the street, kissing and throwing streamers. Naturally, from time to time I went back to our table, on the sidewalk, to drink and smoke, but I was having such a good time I didn't notice anything.

It was only later that someone pointed it out to me:

—Oh! *regarde les amoureux!*

I'm not in the humor for jokes, especially now, knowing how sadly the whole story would end. But it still makes me laugh today to remember how the pair of them looked there, on the sidewalk, among the streamers and the lights. Émilie and Irimia! They sat together, rigid, serious, a little giddy, a little lost, sometimes gazing into each other's eyes. They certainly weren't thinking of anything tender, but the fact that they alone were left at the table out of the whole crowd, neither moving nor talking, united them, at least in our eyes.

I have to confess that I have an instinctive taste for a little cruelty. Not to the point of inflicting torture, but when I'm having a good time I like to find something to make fun of, to make something the secret object of my petty malice. It's vulgar, I admit. But that's the way it is. That evening, I didn't have to invent a target. It forced itself on me. Anyway, all I did was to be present and amused at a game the others—Mado in particular— would have played even without me: getting Émilie to be Irimia's lover. Making them girlfriend and boyfriend. They caressed both of them, dropped hints shamelessly, praised Émilie's beauty and Irimia's strength. The two were slightly bewildered but remained serious, which made the situation even more ridiculous because they indeed took on the air of a bride and groom. Beyond that, Irimia could make no sense of the chatter around him and looked about pathetically, beseechingly; it pains me to remember it today.

It would have gone no further and I would have forgotten all about it in the whirlpool of the celebrations had the skies not suddenly begun to pour rain at about midnight. A real summer storm. Hard and fast. In a flash, the little place de la Sorbonne was deserted, tables knocked over, glasses shattered in the rush. Bits of wet streamers flapped about like autumn leaves. We scattered in all directions and it was all I could do to grab Mado and pull her with me toward home, which wasn't far off. I'd forgotten all about Irimia and Émilie. Nobody who remembers that Fourteenth of July rainstorm would blame me.

But Irimia later told me in detail everything that happened after I left, and, knowing both him and Émilie well, I don't think it's hard to imagine exactly what occurred. Left alone together at the table in the rain, they didn't know how to say goodbye. They didn't know each other, they'd never spoken to one another, they weren't able to talk, and, as a result, they found it hard to get to the point concerning their needs. Taking such a decision was beyond their imagination and power. They were together, were they not? So they had to remain that way, and they set off through the rain without exchanging a word. Her dress was wet and water was pouring off the brim of her hat. He took off his coat and wrapped her in it, pulling her to him, so that they huddled together. He guided her along easily; she hardly came above his waist. They walked like that for hours. I think it's about ten kilometers to Saint-Ouen, where Émilie lives. They covered the whole distance on foot, dragging themselves through those wet, deserted streets. Dawn was breaking when they reached Émilie's door.

How the rest happened, I don't know. How Irimia went upstairs to her garret, how they fell into one another's arms, how they collapsed, clothed, on the floor! It was, perhaps, exhaustion catching up with them, as it does with overworked beasts. It was the dizziness of that evening of music, flashing lights and fireworks. It was the republican

Fourteenth of July, beating with delayed splendor in their hearts, it was the rain caressing their cheeks and "The Marseillaise" still ringing in their ears, in the background, like a romantic song. Or it was the overriding need to say something. They felt an obscure, elementary kinship, like that of one workhorse for another when they pull the same load, and, as they did not have a language in common, in a moment of intuition they found the simplest way to make themselves heard.

But why should I get carried away making assumptions? The fact is, next day, toward evening, Irimia knocked on my door. He had a grave, portentous air. He paced about, as though he wanted to say something but didn't know how to begin. He fiddled with his cap and coughed a few times. Then he just spat it out, the way shy people do when they wander about for an hour with a cup of tea in their hands, not knowing where to set it, and end up just dropping it on the floor.

—Hey, I went to bed with Émilie last night...

I must have looked surprised, because he lowered his eyes, embarrassed. I knew Irimia never lied, but it seemed so abominable that I was wary of believing it. I would have liked to laugh and I even tried.

—You rake! I said, shaking my finger at him in admiration.

He smiled briefly, then resumed his previous portentous expression. He sighed. Then, from the depths of his soul, in a tone of such guilt, which I could not have matched even had I killed someone, confessed:

—And she was a virgin!

And now, this is where my little portion of guilt begins. Because I knew that Émilie Vignou was a virgin. I also knew that in her world this wasn't very significant, and that making love was not a matter of tremendous import. Still, enjoying Irimia's horrified expression, amused by his utter naïveté, I played along. Who knows? Perhaps if at that point I'd taken care to tell Irimia that the matter wasn't so serious, the story might have ended differently. If I hadn't, on the contrary, assumed a preoccupied expression, paced about the room, and stared at him reprovingly, as though he were on trial.

He didn't even dare to meet my reproachful look. He said, simply:

—It doesn't matter. I'll take her.

—What do you mean you'll take her?

—I'll take her as my wife!

I knew he wasn't joking, but I told myself that it wouldn't really come to that in the end. I let him leave, had great amusement at his expense afterward and then forgot about it. A week later a fellow student mentioned that Irimia was getting married. I was stunned. I immediately ran about looking for him, hoping to reach him in time to extricate him from his fix. He turned out to be perfectly calm; the calm of one whose conscience is clear.

I tried to shake him awake, to make him see what he was doing, to persuade him.

—You fool, don't you realize what you're doing? You're poor, you have to get a job, you have to go back to your own country. Your parents are waiting there for you!

—But she was a virgin!

I told him it didn't matter in the least, gave him the example of other fellows who had also known "virgins," and that nothing had befallen them in consequence. I told him that things were a bit different in Paris from how they were in his village. He didn't want to know. He sat there impassively, as though nothing could penetrate that frowning forehead of his.

—But she was a virgin!

That was his verdict, his straitjacketed plowman's sense of honor, and I saw plainly that he would not be shaken from it. I tried then to persuade Émilie. Not that Irimia's fate mattered greatly to me, but such a marriage struck me as monstrous. Humanly speaking, the joining together of this giant and that badly wrought, wooden girl was horrible, beastly. What kind of a life could they have together up there in that garret in Saint-Ouen, communicating with sign language, since they had no common tongue, knowing nothing of one another, growling at each other in place of speech and coupling like dumb curs after nightfall? Émilie, a poor, easily suggestible soul, had received Irimia's proposal without surprise. She didn't really understand why he was so set on marrying her, but she had no reason to reject him. Then there were her friends, for whom this marriage was a great opportunity for sport. They wasted no time in sowing confusion to the point where nobody could have sorted it out. Faced with a fait accompli, I abandoned my objections. I attended the civil wedding ceremony of Émilie Vignou and Irimia C. Irimia exactly fifteen days later. A handful of the groom's supporters were present in that room in the town hall of the Fourteenth Arrondissement and an entire legion of shopgirls, all colleagues of Émilie from the basement of her establishment. They'd come for the fun, but it was a melancholy spectacle. The scene was so absurd it was painful to look at and I don't recall seeing anybody laughing. The girls were weepy. Only Émilie, on her groom's rigid arm, had a modest queenly glow and her usual ugliness shone solemnly, like an aura of chastity.

FOUR

or a long time I heard no more about them. I'd left Paris in August for a small town in the Midi where I worked as a substitute doctor. I returned late, in November, with tens of thousands of francs and the wife of the doctor I'd substituted for, a pathetic, ugly woman. (But that's another story...) I had of course split up with Mado by that stage; the relationship had in any case dragged on too long. So I was no longer in contact with anyone who could give me news about Mr. and Mrs. Irimia.

But I saw them one Sunday in the Jardin des Plantes, looking at the animals. They were holding hands, the way the soldiers and housemaids do in the Cişmigiu Gardens in Bucharest, a sad reminder for me in that Parisian park of our down-at-heel neighborhoods back home. They stopped in the middle of a group of children in front of the elephant pen. From his overcoat pocket, Irimia took out a piece of bread wrapped in paper. He unwrapped it and shared it with the giant beasts.

He cooed to them in Romanian:

—Come on, that's a nice fellow!

Each time an elephant's trunk passed between the bars and swayed in the air, then came down toward Irimia, Émilie jumped with fright and tried to pull him away, but he stood there calmly. He was having a good time with the animals and they seemed to accept him. I held back from them, not wishing to disturb this peaceful scene. But I saw them again three months later, in tragic circumstances. I'm used to death and have had occasion to close the eyes of the dead in those white-painted hospital wards where I spent my youth, while thinking of other things besides the bodies decomposing there, in front of me. What do you expect? It's professional detachment, and leaves no room for the fear of the end. But Émilie's death shook me badly. It was barbaric.

One day in March, Irimia came looking for me at the hotel, asking me to find a bed in my ward for Émilie, who was pregnant and would soon give birth.

—All right, Irimia. But is that what you really need now? Kids? Why didn't you take care of it when there was time?

Irimia seemed not to understand. He looked at me, confused, and when he understood that I was talking about an abortion made the sign of the cross automatically. I wasn't involved with obstetrics at Trousseau, but I told Irimia that I'd make arrangements through the management and try to get the necessary bed. And indeed, it was sorted out within two days. The intern in maternity was a friend of mine and promised to take good care of Émilie. As for myself, when I wasn't on duty and had a break from my own patients I went across to ward 18, to lend a hand.

I was certain from the moment I brought Émilie in that she would not leave there alive. I had never seen such a pregnancy. It wasn't abnormal, clinically speaking; her vital signs were fine and she was a good patient. But her entire body was misshapen. An enormous belly, her limbs heavy and projecting stiffly from her body. Her breathing was labored and sometimes her eyes rolled upward in their sockets, like a goose that's been force-fed. That lumpy body that creaked like an unoiled pulley. That asymmetrical body, without the reflexes required to carry within it another body, a child! It was an absurdity, a physical impossibility. Émilie—for whom picking up a glass of water and setting it down in a different place was a balancing act—now had to give birth to a child! Her rigid body would have had to yield to the infant's struggling within, to surrender to its blind wormlike writhing.

It was butchery. She lay like an overturned barrel. If she could have twisted about she might have suffered less, and might have made it, possibly. But no, she lay rigid in the bed and looked up at us from there with anxious, beseeching eyes, like a drowning dog. From time to time she screamed and her howls could be heard from afar, through the main wards, just as the lowing of slaughtered cattle must be heard in abattoirs. We considered getting the forceps ready but the head doctor, whom I'd brought to the patient's bedside, would not permit it. He said she was finished in any case. It went on for three days and nights. Irimia, whom I wanted to send away, remained there by his wife's bed throughout and stubbornly resisted my entreaties. I'd never seen such determination. He sat still, saying nothing, not even sighing, looking sometimes at me and sometimes at Émilie and waiting.

On the third night, at three a.m., she gave birth to a baby girl. Irimia took her from my hands. He brought her close to a light, gazed at her, then gave her to one of the nurses and went away to get some sleep. When I returned next day to the hospital, he was at Émilie's bedside. She was in agony. She'd been hemorrhaging badly from early morning and septicemia had set in. She was snoring. Seeing me, Irimia put his finger to his lips to tell me to be quiet.

—She's on the mend now, he said. She's made it through.

I didn't have the courage to reply. Misinterpreting the grave look on my face, he continued:

—That thing she's doing with her mouth? It's nothing: it's just a tic. Then, unable to contain his pride at being a father: "A little girl? What do you say to that? Have you seen what a beauty she is? Come see her." And he dragged me after him, into a nearby ward.

Émilie died toward evening on the following day. I don't know who closed her eyes. We buried her one bright, sunny morning at the end of March. It was warm and I went out without my overcoat, smiling in that white spring light. On the way there, flower girls were setting out little bouquets of lilies of the valley for a franc each and I bought them all up in memory of Émilie. Irimia wore his formal black coat, the same one he'd worn nine months earlier at his wedding. Mado was in a corner of the cemetery, as I'd never seen her before, looking distraught and crying like a child, convulsively, and when she spotted me from afar she smiled at me through her tears. She was a nice, sentimental sort of girl.

Maria

ONE

Your sudden declaration yesterday both surprised and troubled me. I wasn't expecting it, believe me. I was certain that things were clear-cut and unambiguous between us and on those occasions when I leaned on your shoulder (though this gesture always infuriates Andrei) I did it in a friendly, whimsical fashion, almost without realizing I was doing it, just like so many other gestures of familiarity.

So why have you turned out like the rest of them? Allow me to reprimand you. You deserve it and I'll also enjoy administering it. And don't for a second interpret my silence and my abrupt exit from the ball as the indignation of an outraged woman. I'm old already, though you don't want to believe that, and I've heard the words you spoke last night so many times before—in other circumstances, perhaps in other variants—that such an occurrence no longer strikes me as curious and I take it with a lighthearted shrug. Yes, lighthearted.

So don't curse me for having frowned at you yesterday. You haven't done anything wrong. I just think our wonderful friendship could have done without this accident and that your loving me or wishing to love me or thinking you love me is an unnecessary complication in a relationship which I value and for a long time believed possible. Look, you've done such a job of messing things up that I wonder if it's prudent to tell you I was fond of you and always looked forward tremendously to your visits. You're an idiot—that's what you are!

Yesterday, when you'd finished talking, I suddenly felt that something was over, had got too complicated, and it annoyed me so much I felt I could no longer stay in that ballroom and I asked Andrei to take me home, though I knew this would bother him, as he'd been deep in conversation with Suzy Ioaniu and was probably hoping to dance the night away with her. (It only occurred to me later that Andrei might have thought I was making a jealous scene by leaving early, thereby indirectly flattering Suzy, which of course upset me, but it was too late to fix that and in the end it didn't really matter anyway. To tell the truth, tearing them apart might even have given me some satisfaction.)

Now, let's be straight with each other, like two sensible people. The Brailowski concert is on at the Atheneum on Monday evening and, as neither of us would miss it (at least I hope you won't be so foolish), we'll see each other there. Well, I don't want us to be afraid to shake hands, or to be glancing sideways at each other, or having awkward conversations about the weather, with the feeling that we have a secret. On the contrary. At the end of the concert I want you, just as before, to offer to see me home. I think I'll be on my own because, as you know, Andrei doesn't like music and in any case on Monday evening he'll be at Suzy's, rehearsing a sketch for the revue for Prince Mircea in which he, Andrei, plays the king of tango.

It's hard, perhaps, to explain ourselves and I wonder if I have the courage to write this letter to the end, but I can't, I truly can't, burden my already overcomplicated life with yet another secret, yet another strange situation. In my little world, you are the only man I can speak freely with and I don't plan to lose that. Sometimes I—accustomed as I am to the little lies I and others tell—have a longing for sincerity that brings me to tears. I feel smothered by all the little compromises my life is made of and it makes me want to fight back—uselessly, foolishly—by telling once and for all the truth, the whole truth, holding nothing back, indifferent to whatever might happen next. Sometimes, toward evening, when you came and had tea with me, I didn't plan to speak to you about it. But you're a logical gentleman and your replies put me off. You know, if at times I seized the chance to offer you the box of cigarettes or the plate with cookies, though you already had a cigarette and some cakes, I performed these useless gestures in order to change the subject or resist the temptation to.

But today I'm not going to mince my words. Do you know I love Andrei? Don't tell me I'm choosing the wrong moment: you don't need to be treated with kid gloves, I don't have that kind of finesse. The only thing that matters is for us to be clear with one another. I've heard that people refer to my relationship with Andrei as a casual sort of thing: an "arrangement" which has lasted five years and will sooner or later come to an end. Perhaps that is why women permit themselves to flirt with Andrei in front of me and why men talk to me rather freely when they get me on my own. Perhaps that's why you tend to say harsh things about him and, in front of me, give him little ironic smiles. He may deserve them, but they hurt me. Because, in the end, you're naive. You believe in intelligence, good taste, discretion, subtlety, and beyond all that you don't understand how somebody could possibly love Andrei. Yes, Andrei, your friend and my lover. More than once I've caught you smiling with disbelief when I went up to him to stand by his side or say something to him in private. Maybe you told yourself that all there was to that beautiful man was fooling about with jazz and spending two hours every morning arranging his hair, and that in his bedroom he had a pinup of Rudolph Valentino cut out from some movie magazine. I'm not proud, but in those moments I would have liked to have gone up to you and told you that you're dull and conceited and what bothers you is that he's so much handsomer than you. Your superiority pains me. When you say something intelligent, it feels as though you're reprimanding me. I would have liked to tell you that I'm aware of this. That I know Andrei just as well as you do, and it doesn't change a thing.

I once told you how Andrei finished second in a tennis tournament. You flicked the ash from your cigarette, looked at me, and said casually, in passing, "Missed the top spot!"

I hated you that day. Because, you know, you force me to judge a feeling which I entertained in a simple, undemanding way. You were like a botanist intent on demonstrating that the laws of science required me to dislike a flower that I liked. You were the first person to make me ask myself why I loved Andrei, which is a completely irrelevant question and gets us nowhere.

Why do I love him? Good God! Because it was meant to be that way! I met him a year after the divorce. I was in no mood for crazy passion. I was taking pleasure in dressing and inventing my own outfits for the days of travel and sunshine. I was preparing to leave but was unable to decide between the coast and the mountains, and kept putting off my departure from one week to the next, even though Bucharest was beginning to bore me. Then Andrei turned up. He courted me with the devilish impudence of a theatrical young suitor, and it amused me, just as it must amuse the Prince of Wales to be accosted by strangers in the street who are ignorant of his identity and ask him the time or for a small favor. I laughed and, for fun, encouraged him. Because I couldn't in any case tell this likable, enterprising, self-confident person that he was mistaken: "Whom do you take me for, sir?" is a formal response. I like to be taken for exactly who people think I am.

Perhaps if then, in the first days of that spring, I'd known where the joke was going, I would have cut it short. I close my eyes and, without any regrets, wonder how my life would have turned out. What sweet silence, what warm tiredness!

Andrei entered my life in a moment of inattention, when I'd left the doors open and the shutters up. You know him: you can't guard against him. He isn't difficult, he isn't bad, he isn't good, he isn't simple, and he isn't complicated. Evening falls, it's dark in the bedroom, you tiredly switch on the lamp and, in the sudden brightness, in a corner, there's Andrei.

—You were here?

Yes, he was there. And since he happened to be there and because you're tired and it's late, you ask him to do you a little favor, to call the maid, to get you a book from the shelf, to tell you if he liked the green dress you were wearing the previous day, to pull the tea table a little closer, to hum the melody you heard last night at the Modern that you've forgotten.

Summer slipped away, spent in the enjoyment of these little pleasures. One day I looked at the calendar and it was August 15. Now it was too late to leave Bucharest. The evenings were hot and muggy, with an enervating undercurrent of tension. Andrei found me by the window, my forehead pressed against the glass, as back in my adolescent days when I was home alone, not expecting any visitors, looking out from the balcony, past my neighborhood, past the city, for something that was surely on its way, though I knew not what. I told him I no longer planned to leave. He was voluble, enthusiastic, he kissed my hands, fell to his knees, rose and did a pirouette—all of which he could get away with because it was part of a joke:

—*Madame, ma voiture vous attend!*

He waved toward the door, smiling, young, and gallant, and the invitation in French reminded me of a phrase I'd often heard people using affectionately when referring to him: *Ce cher André.* I laughed and took his arm, like a friend, and went down. In those days he had a little Chenard Torpedo, which if I recall rightly he wrote off two years ago in Italy when we had that accident in the Alps. He got behind the wheel, drove off with me with an arrogant little smile that suited him very well back then and also intimidated me somehow.

I'm writing quickly, without reading back over what I've written. Telling you all this, I have a distinct feeling of how obscene it all is. Yes, I became Andrei's lover with the complicity of an automobile, an August evening, and a smile. I, who retain from love a bitter memory of time wasted, should not perhaps have the right to regret plunging into passion like that, through a side door. Still, I think sometimes of a love that is solemn and begins cleanly and clearly, with a kind of secret wedding between me and a man—which is perhaps only the result of my good bourgeois upbringing and which amuses me, but it might also be something else, something harder to explain.

I wasn't intoxicated that evening and I think I've never let myself go completely, which I actually despise about myself, because I wish I could have lived such pleasant, frivolous moments free of the constraints of good taste, but at the very moment I rested my head on Andrei's shoulder, let myself go in the blowing wind, I told myself it was just a harmless bit of vaudeville.

The lights became fewer after Otopeni. Andrei took a small, portable flashlight from his dashboard and handed it to me so I could illuminate the curves of the road. It was utterly entrancing. All I had before me was the white strip of the headlights, then a stretch of inky blackness, and then far beyond that a patch of incandescence made by the flashlight I was holding. Applying gentle pressure with two fingers, I maneuvered this unsteady light and followed how it fell on a rock a kilometer away, on a hanging branch, on the base of a bridge. I looked intently ahead, peering through the dark for unexpected twists in the road. It was an intense task. All I had was the sharp, immediate sense of my own tension: around me was the nervous tempo of the motor, the man sitting confidently beside me and steering, the black, rustling trees sweeping past on both sides, the silver dials near the brake, and perhaps still—distant-feeling, fabulous—the surrounding light. And now, leaning over my page at this little table, remembering that trip, I can feel the same pulsation beneath my temple.

It was late, I don't know how late, or where it was, when Andrei braked hard. The lights from a few scattered houses nearby shone through the trees.

—*Madame, la nuit vous attend.*

It was beautiful, the way he said it. Don't laugh. The way he said it, it was like the chorus from some melody with awful lyrics which you sing anyway and enjoy because they're beautiful in the passing moment. You're far too intelligent to be able to understand that. I followed him.

TWO

We stayed there for two weeks. It was a village beyond Câmpina, not so far from Sinaia. I still don't know what it's called. I wanted to return to Bucharest the next morning. I told Andrei, the way you'd tell someone at a party, after midnight, that it's late and you want to leave. He laughed and shrugged.

—We can't!

—Andrei, be reasonable. It's been lovely, but I have to leave now!

—In what?

—In your automobile.

—It's broken.

—There was nothing wrong with it yesterday.

—And today there is. Automobiles are temperamental things...

—You're kidding me.

—No, I swear. This morning—you were still asleep—I went out to the yard and smashed the carburetor. I don't like to take chances. It occurred to me that you might want to run off. And I decided that our adventure had to be defended against everybody, against yourself above all. Believe me: a functioning automobile is a dangerous thing. A broken-down one, forty kilometers from a town, you can rely upon. I've wrecked mine.

—You're crazy!

—Indeed.

Andrei's style in this exchange will be familiar to you. That style which you described as cordial and ingenuous, by which you surely meant to say he was boorish and conceited, but which I liked then and still do today. You see, even today, after the accumulated fatigue of the past five years and with the cruelty I've patiently learned from him, I can't stop smiling when I remember that daring, happy, reckless, cocksure Andrei who took me prisoner, proud of what he'd pulled off. He was wearing white summer trousers and his shirtsleeves were rolled up and his collar open, which gave him a youthful look, and in that country yard, something of a simple, joyful, rustic air.

I've told you that I'm old. I was then too. Not as old as now, but old all the same. There's been a weariness in me for a very long time. I don't know the reason for it, but it makes me sensitive to anything involving images of courage, to sudden gestures, to daring speech, to the face of an impetuous young man. I don't know. It must be something like the melancholy of summer's end, when the sun is still strong and the light is clear but the tops of the evening trees shiver with a presentiment of the coming decline, a knowledge it contains within itself the way a loaf of bread recalls the hot embers of the fire where it was baked.

Andrei won me that morning. He won me over, won my heart, and the meaning of that expression became clear to me that morning in a way it hadn't when I'd come across it in the cinema and the theater, probably so that the revelation could be total for me later on.

I shook his hand, agreeing to everything. He embraced me noisily and with immense childish enthusiasm, but at the same time controlling his display—which I didn't dislike. I don't ever mind giving people I'm fond of the impression that a whim of theirs is an order. I don't remember with what degree of irony I went along with him. There must have been some. Very little, though: just the amount I needed to excuse myself for my lack of what you would call "restraint." I discarded my restraint the way you'd discard an uncomfortable hat in order to feel the wind blowing through your hair.

—Even so, we can't stay here.

—Why not?

—Simple. All I have is this dress I'm wearing and you've that one suit.

He smiled, kissed me, threw his jacket over his shoulder, and took off, shouting that he'd be back by lunchtime. He ran the several kilometers to the main road, stopped the first car that appeared, surprised the driver by jumping in, and was in Brasov in an hour. He rushed through the town and in another hour was back, laden with packages, boxes, and bags which we opened together, laughing at the discovery of each purchase, as he didn't really know what he'd brought either and every item was a surprise for both of us: pyjamas, a gramophone with a single record, a wool dress, sports clothes, candy, books, a Ping-Pong set, hand-kerchiefs, powders, eau de cologne, sunglasses—a fantastic bazaar composed of charming trifles, assembled with stun-ning bad taste.

It's a stupid thing to say to you and probably inappro-priate, but you'll forgive me this moment of sentiment: they were the most wonderful days I can remember. I have a whole stack of photographs from that time and I often look at them—even today—without regret, without complaint for everything that's happened since, happy to discover some new detail in one of those pictures I know by heart and in which everything, absolutely everything, is affecting: his white shoes, my broken sandal strap (I'd been running a lot and had snagged it in a hollow in the ground one day coming back from Prahova, where we'd been bathing in a secluded spot, utterly naked, because we didn't have swim-ming costumes and also just for the joy the madness gave us), and everything is intact, recent, amicable—how can I describe it?—not like a desperate evocation of something lost, rather the leisurely, relaxed recognition of a landscape you inhabit and feel will always be yours.

Since then Andrei has, on numerous occasions, been brutal, obscene, and mean, but all this and much else—immeasurably more than I'd tell you about, not because I fear you or because I'd find it humiliating (I haven't had that kind of pride for years) but because it would make me sick to list it all—turns to nothing when I remember those two weeks at the beginning.

I think I mentioned that there was a gramophone player and a record among all the things brought from Brasov. Just one record. I don't know why he'd got hold of just one and why it was that one. On one side was a Hungarian dance by Brahms and on the other a Spanish dance by Granados, both played on the violin by Jascha Heifetz. It was a red His Master's Voice record and I can still see it perfectly, though for some reason I haven't bothered to look for it since. For two weeks, in the morning, at lunchtime, and in the evening—mostly in the evening, after dinner—waiting on the veranda for midnight, we listened to those two melodies, which became so familiar to us that they ceased being pieces of music and became a kind of domestic ritual, an integral part of our life there, similar to all the other household sounds—familiar footfalls on the porch, the ticking of the clock on the wall, the noise of a door opening and shutting.

See, so many years have passed, I've forgotten so much and will forget so much more, but I think I'll always remember those songs. Not because they're beautiful—I don't even know if they are—but because the holiday is contained so deeply within them that not even Andrei, who only knows tangos, has ever forgotten them and he sometimes, without even realizing it, finds himself humming one of them while he's eating or smiling.

I'd love not to know what they're called or where I heard them, and for him to take them away with him nicely, as you'd carry off a forgotten letter from last year in the inside pocket of your overcoat, a letter you thought you'd lost. Anyway, I've never asked him anything about that.

THREE

We got back to Bucharest late, at the end of September, and found that everybody else had returned from their trips long before us and the trees along the road were turning yellow. It was then that I met you also, you were just back from Paris, having studied medicine of some kind, and Andrei commented skeptically to me about this ("That Stefan Valeriu will never do anything serious"), and perhaps you remember how embarrassing it was for me that day, when he called out to you in the street so he could introduce me to you, and how he was bursting with pride and suggestiveness. I felt he expected to be congratulated for me and for his "conquest." I felt how gratified he was by my dress, my eyes, and your amazement.

How I struggled in those days to temper his enthusiasm and indiscretion! I wasn't a prudent person and don't think I am today. But I was alarmed by the rumors, assumptions, and comments, and by the opening nights when I felt a trail of whispering behind me as I passed through the foyer. Or when I entered a restaurant and was met with thirty pairs of eyes that had heard something and wanted the whole story. The awkward questions, the innuendo... If I could have distributed a circular to everybody confirming that I was Andrei's mistress and been sure that this would have satisfied public curiosity, I would have done it. I was weary of the whiff of scandal preceding me wherever I went.

I tried explaining all this to Andrei. I told him I wasn't ashamed in front of anybody, but that we needed to give our love time to find its appropriate "social formula" (I don't think this horrible term was employed, but that was what I meant). I asked him to let things be, to let them settle.

—You're a bourgeois, was his reply.

I didn't get annoyed. In a way, he was right. He was impassioned, expansive, and buzzing with plans for the future; I was reserved and a little skeptical. Lucid, at least. I enjoyed his friendship, but was tired of his juvenile effusiveness. I insisted on one thing specifically: that we live apart. I wouldn't concede on that point. He was reckless, domineering, and threatening by turns, but I was unyielding and that was the end of the matter.

—But for God's sake why not live together? You let me sleep at your place. You have me over for dinner. You come out with me in town. So why not live together? Why not move in with me? Why not get a bigger place, for both of us?

It would have been hard to say why and hard for him to understand. I didn't even try. But I remained firm. I needed my own home, where I could be alone: a room where nobody could enter without knocking, a chest where

I could lock away whatever I wished, four walls between which I could gather myself, at a remove from the world. A "fortress mentality" was how you described it once and I didn't know what to say. But don't think that's what it is! I just know that I like my interior life, that my greatest pleasure is to return to it in the evening, and I've retained a very clear idea of home as a "refuge" (the return of the prodigal son is the only passage in the Bible that has ever moved me). If I haven't ever let my life go to pieces, it's largely thanks to this room in which I'm writing to you today. By being here, I've held myself back so many times from doing crazy things, from losing my temper, from leaping before I looked...And the number of times I've returned here wounded, anxiety written on my face, my arms hanging by my side, unable to make sense of some disaster which had engulfed me, thinking my life was over. When you'd see me in the street a day or two later, I'd smile to myself, thinking how much personal damage lies beneath my calm exterior. Because you would congratulate me for my calmness and I was proud of it—for reasons other than those you imagine, believe me.

The house is the only thing I kept for myself. The rest, bit by bit, fell under Andrei's control. He knew how to ask for things and he had a spoiled child's instinct for grabbing them. I liked his agitated appearance, the way he sounded tense and peremptory, the way he'd throw his hat off as he stood in the doorway, his flurry of questions, his curt replies, the way he paced the room, picking up objects and setting them down somewhere else, amazed at everything, wanting to know everything, impatient, intolerant and tyrannical and full of himself.

—Andrei, you're outrageous!

I was kidding him. He'd suddenly feel powerful and commanding and he'd smile at me arrogantly—a smile I liked immensely, because I became restrained and passive while he became reckless and presumptuous. I knew from the start he was vain, but I was happy to cultivate this, because it was his most sensitive point. It made him impossible sometimes but it also gave him a certain rough grace, like an adolescent who knows no boundaries. Privately, I felt I was the stronger of the two of us, and I often thought that most of his victories over me, at least at the beginning, were really little concessions I'd made so he wouldn't have to go off in a sulk.

It's hard to say when exactly I came to depend on Andrei. There probably wasn't a precise moment. My love for him grew gradually, out of an accretion of moments and habits, until one day I found I was his prisoner. For a long time I considered myself free and regarded him with detachment and, because I could judge him coldly and was aware of all his amusing failings, I was naive enough to consider myself independent of him and capable of splitting up with him at any moment, at no great cost to myself. I could never have imagined that man, with his rages and fantasies of control, could ever cause suffering to me, the one who regarded him so indulgently and ironically. I had the impression he was playing at being a tyrant with me and I was playing along, answering back like a slave, the way grown-ups act scared when a child with a sheet over its head says *hoo-hooo* like a monster...

I had no idea what a dangerous game I was playing.

FOUR

Our first bad fight was because of my name, which Andrei doesn't like at all. He found it hard to address me by it properly, as it is, plain and common and without any personality. But it's my name, I was given it when I was little: Maria. When we were on our own together he tried all kinds of variations and affectionate diminutives, which I firmly rejected.

—I'm warning you, Andrei. If you call me by anything other than by my real name, I won't answer.

But his suffering began when he had to introduce me to somebody new and, counting on my embarrassment, corrected my name, pronouncing the English or French versions or dropping the first syllable.

He called me, by turn, Marie, Mary, and Ria. And every time he tried it, I thwarted him calmly, which infuriated him.

—My name is Maria. Andrei likes to say it differently; an old joke of his.

Don't laugh: it was an important matter and in the end I managed to prevail, because I suspected this was the crux of the difference between us, the surest sign that we were from two different worlds.

Why did he dislike "Maria"? I'm not entirely sure. I asked him a few times and he couldn't explain it.

—Look, he said, all the women we know have normal names. Suzy Ioaniu, for example. Her name's Suzana, but admit it, it would be horrible to call her Suzana. Then there's Bebe Stoian. And Anny. Everybody, in other words: Lulu, Lily, Ritta, Gaby... Except you... Maria—what a provincial name!

I laughed. I was genuinely amused by his passion for fancy, funny, cute names you could write with a y or a silent e, or with a double consonant. Names the easygoing aesthete Andrei may have picked up from nightclub shows and which he wished to apply to my own dull, provincial, three-syllable name, which I was used to and liked, because it was so simple and common. How triumphant Andrei was when he arrived at my place and discovered that my new maid was also a Maria. He didn't even have to laugh; he just extended his hand, palm open, as though to say, behold the evidence, I rest my case. Good God, what a face he made when I told him it didn't bother me in the slightest and that there was no reason to trouble with my name or that of the maid, it would do fine for both of us and all the other Marias in the world. He ended the conversation sharply:

—You're an incorrigible bourgeois. You might as well wear a dress from 1915, to go with your name.

Much later, only two years ago, in Paris, in circumstances that will make you laugh but which I found really moving, Andrei agreed in the end that my name was no better or worse than any other and even suited me well. We were visiting galleries in the rue Boétie, and at the Bernheim-Jeune happened across an odd exhibition by the Italian actress Maria Lani, who knew many famous artists personally and had them paint her portrait, thereby assembling a collection of extraordinary paintings.

I think Andrei was surprised that a woman as distinguished as that Italian actress could be called Maria. I also think he was proud we bore the same name, and I remember him looking at me several times in the exhibition with a flicker of the admiration he hadn't shown me for a very long time, and perhaps hasn't since.

We dined somewhere in Montmartre that evening in a modest, cheerful bar and Andrei was his old, playful, vibrant, direct self and talked a lot of charming nonsense.

—Maria, I've been a fool and it's unforgivable. Your name suits you perfectly. A name lacking obvious charm, a name which can't stand diminutives, proud like you, simple like you, perhaps a little too serious, because sometimes I wish you were different, livelier, more edgy. Not like me, because I'm completely nuts, but different in any case...

—Younger, Andrei, younger, I said, helping him to formulate the thought.

He protested vehemently, pointed out that he was older than me, mentioned his gray hairs, but despite his protests I know I'd spoken the truth and that evening Andrei, whom you laugh at for his puffed-up, conceited talk, had said the most sensitive and perceptive things that could be said about our agitated love affair. I thought then, after I don't know how many months of resignation, that my relationship with Andrei was not irretrievably compromised, as long as such a moment of understanding was possible, and that—who knows?—with a little patience and a certain determination at times, and a bit of luck in the end, I could eventually discover exactly the pedal that needed to be pressed in that emotional game of ours for the harmony we felt that evening to last. To last! You see, that must have been my greatest mistake, not only in my relationship with Andrei, but with everybody else and with life itself. To last! It terrifies me to think that something can be completely obliterated, that a thing or a person or a feeling or even just something familiar can disappear overnight. What obsesses me about ephemeral things is their eternal possibility, the suggestion that they might endure. What was heartbreaking for me about Andrei's company was his continual air of temporariness, like a man who'd walked into a house with his hat on, not knowing if he was staying or leaving. I was ridiculously tempted sometimes to put my hand on his shoulder and to ask him in all seriousness:

—Is that you?

Don't imagine that my desire for permanence was oppressive or even demanded anything of me. I was well aware that Andrei had to keep moving, to betray and—how can I explain?—I think his vaguely vagabondish demeanor stirred something in me and that was exactly why I loved him, because he was scurrying about and engaged in the world while I believed in waiting and eternity. A cheap eternity, certainly, mine and his, but which has to be defended so carefully against so many things! Perhaps his noisy, capricious, and unstable behavior and the way he acted like a domineering, intimidating playboy was something I liked and needed because it was a fresh breeze blowing through what he called my "serious" life. And perhaps he too needed my calmness, at least for the respite it gave him if nothing else, as he found it pleasant to enjoy a day or a week of peace next to me sometimes when his dizzying whims and schemes and escapades had worn him out. Perhaps a dull, excessively bourgeois peace, but one he could count on.

I think that's what Andrei understood in the end, that evening in Paris. Walking home late, through backstreets and along the quays of the Seine, tipsy on wine and anticipation of the night of love we'd silently promised ourselves, I was happy on his arm.

FIVE

What else? I wonder if there's anything else to tell
you. Now that I've got talking about so many
past events which of course I'd never forgotten
for a moment though I'd kept them locked away inside me,
as in a drawer you'd rather not rummage through, I admit
I've got the taste for it. Having dug up so many facts and
regrets and errors, I find talking about it pleasantly painful
in a way, like removing the bandages from an arm long
imprisoned by them. But I'm not going to tell you all the
other stories—the fights and betrayals and explanations—
because I feel it's too late to go over all that ground again.
I've accepted these things for a long time now, the things
that have happened and those that are yet to happen,
and I try to make their comradely presence into a familiar
comfort—probably the only one I have left. Anyway, you
know about it all, just as I do and everybody else does, since
Andrei has held back nothing in making a public display of
every new affair from start to finish.

Do you remember how he ran away to Paris in 1924 with
Didi, that blond starlet who left with him in the middle
of her show's season, leaving a hole in the Carabus revue

and stunning all Bucharest? I'm told it's still talked about today and that their escapade has attained legendary status in the theater world. Meanwhile, I'd go out, make visits, receive visitors—with ridiculous equanimity, with a smile that wasn't faked, with detachment that was immune to the harshest innuendo. How did I do it? I don't know. Was I being funny? Contemptuous? Unfeeling? I swear, I have no idea, but I think I felt the whole ugly business had nothing to do with me, didn't affect me, couldn't affect me, that a solid wall stood between what was going on and who I was.

Nobody understood anything, and Andrei understood less than anybody. He avoided meeting me for two weeks after he returned. He acknowledged me by sending vague messages and nervous go-betweens. Then he turned up at my place one morning, out of the blue, disoriented and not knowing how to proceed, whether to explain himself or to blame me, but wanting in any case to justify himself. I didn't provide him with the opportunity. I received him as though nothing had happened, as if he'd left my home the previous evening, I was friendly, made him laugh and joined in myself, had him stay for dinner, asked him dozens of silly questions. After dinner, I played a few gramophone records that I'd bought for him when he was away, Argentinian tangos, and asked him to show me a dance step that was coming into fashion at the time and which I hadn't managed to catch. This pleased him greatly because he was gratified to be back on his own territory and I felt how this insignificant thing instantly gave him his self-confidence back. He stopped acting guilty and reassumed that air of being in control that we know so well. In the evening, over tea, probably because he likes cakes (you know, those creamy rolls), he looked up from his cup and said amiably:

—You're not my kind of woman, but you're a nice girl.

I looked at him, frowning for the first time. Although I wasn't annoyed, this adjective seemed too light to describe shoulders such as mine, which had proven capable of bearing so much.

—You too, Andrei. You're nice too.

I watched him as he ate in front of me, at the table he'd been absent from for so long. He was greedy, cheerful, and communicative, with a candor that suited him wonderfully and an absence of self-awareness that would have been an excuse for any crime or betrayal. I had always enjoyed watching Andrei eating and I think his greed is the only truly good thing in him, because (maybe I'm talking nonsense, but I'll tell you anyway) there's something childlike about a greedy man, something which tempers his roughness and self-importance and reduces the intimidating aspect of his masculinity. It's possible that simple, stupid women have managed to live their entire lives with great men, kings, generals, and geniuses just because they ate their dinners with them and had the image before them of petulant, hungry children and it was the only thing that made their majesty tolerable.

Oh, there was nothing regal about Andrei, of course, though he could be a petty tyrant in his own way, and my only moment of superiority over him, the only situation in which I felt him dependent on me, when it seemed he expected me to protect him and decide for him, was at dinner, shaking out his napkin, asking with his eyes what I was about to serve him. I know what I'm telling you now is silly and you won't understand any of it, but don't trouble yourself, it's entirely my fault for telling you, a man, things that only a woman could understand and feel.

It's one of the few pleasures for which I'm indebted to Andrei—the pleasure of serving him, waiting on him, watching him preening himself, behind his energetic male facade, indulging his tastes, guiding them. He submitted with the satisfaction of a man who was getting everything he wanted, because he feels entitled to everything and there was something fine in the way he let me take care of him.

I think it was the only thing that really made him feel connected to me, and I knew that no matter how far he ran away or with whom or to where, he would eventually grow tired and head back to me, knowing there was a place where a docile female body awaited him, and a familiar bed, a decent meal, and a gramophone with new tango records.

You know, I'm not ashamed to say that throughout all this I counted on his laziness, on his being greedy and getting tired, and perhaps still, sometimes, on his vanity, as I was an elegant woman—wasn't I?—who looked good on a man's arm on theater opening nights or at a restaurant. That's why I never panicked during any of Andrei's escapades and never ran off to look for him. I was sure he'd be back eventually. I'm not saying it wasn't hard, especially in the early days. The number of times I waited in vain for him when I'd invited him to dinner and he'd promised to come, the number of evenings I was dressed for a show, waiting for the doorbell to ring, watching the time slip away—ten more minutes, five more, until I finally realized he wasn't coming and changed out of my clothes, not indignantly, but sad that I'd wasted an evening. And how stupid I felt telling the maid I'd be breakfasting alone, when I'd already instructed her to set the table for two, or when I didn't go out and she'd seen me getting ready for the theater or a walk only a little earlier. Perhaps you have never experienced such little indignities or known what weariness they cause, but, having lived daily with them, I would have honestly preferred a serious incident involving terrible pain that hits you head-on and either knocks you over or forces you to change.

I never asked Andrei for explanations and I stopped him whenever he tried to give me any, as I knew that nothing could have eradicated my deep feeling of doubt and the rest—facts, arguments, justifications—is of no interest. Besides, the pleasure of seeing him again was so fresh and vivid each time that everything else disappeared, while he was with me at least. Do you remember when we met on

Calea Victoriei one morning this spring, during the general election, and you said you'd just seen Andrei, who was going that evening to Turda, where he was running as a candidate? I gave you a simple response, as though I knew all about Andrei's presence in Bucharest and his departure for Turda. In fact, I didn't know anything, and I hadn't seen Andrei for nearly a month at that point. He'd mentioned his candidacy the last time we'd met and I hadn't approved of it, as I considered it too serious a prank for him. So, he was in Bucharest! Walking about, talking to people, having a good time...I suddenly missed him and was so dejected that there was no room for regrets or for fighting it, just the timid hope that I'd see him too, and hear him talking and clasp his hand.

After dinner I went to the station and arrived an hour early, which frightened me because it occurred to me in the meantime that Andrei might have passed by my place and not found me at home. I waited on the platform, beside the first carriage so that I could see the whole length of the train and be sure not to miss him in the bustling crowd. He arrived late, only a few minutes before the train departed, and when he saw me from afar he stopped dead, out of surprise or fear. Probably because he expected a scene. I gave him a little reassuring wave and he approached with exaggerated cheerfulness, forcing himself to be chatty, which was unnecessary, because all I wanted was to see him. He was sweet and affectionate and—standing in the open doorway of the train, hanging on the railing—kept squeez-ing my hand and speaking effusively, but at the same time impatient for the departure whistle. I thought then that by some miracle he might suddenly leap down, and with his case in one hand and my arm in the other we would head for the exit, him telling me he was going to spend the night in Bucharest. For a moment the idea of asking him to do this flashed through my mind, but fortunately I bit my lip and smiled and said nothing. The train started moving and Andrei waved extravagantly from the steps until he was far away, beaming with satisfaction and pride, while I tottered before a chasm, knowing only that I must not cry. Perhaps that moment sums up all that happened between us.

SIX

t's late, isn't it? Too late for regrets and reproaches. If Andrei hadn't come along... Well, let's face it, I don't know what might have been had Andrei not come along. He occupied my existence so completely, filled it up as you'd furnish an abandoned house. His silhouette, like a boxer's, has blocked so many doorways that might have led else-where, toward other people and situations, that now when I try to imagine what might have been without him, all I see is an immense void. I sense I wouldn't have been so weary and wouldn't have had this feeling of desolation that I use as a shield, but beyond that, beyond Andrei's absence, I can see nothing. I've tried sometimes, and am trying tonight, after your extraordinary declaration yesterday evening, to compose myself somewhat and to judge coldly my love for this person, whom I of course know and have no illusions about. I have a sharp sense of what's proper and what's not, a kind of instinct for simple justice between people, and I told myself there's something unfair in my relationship with Andrei, that there are things in me that would have flourished in the hands of another, qualities I have that are neither stunning nor invaluable but that might have brightened the life of the man I loved. I tell myself that all these things are too heavy or too light for Andrei, that he has no use for them, and that by staying with him I'm wasting a life that could be of value somewhere else, to somebody else, and that this perhaps knocks the entire universe out of kilter, because in the final account this missing stock of love will be discovered.

Silly, isn't it? But not as silly, if you can believe it, as being overwhelmed by the fear of losing my true vocation. Sometimes, in Andrei's company, I find myself terrified of the thought of finding that I'm a prisoner and that somewhere, I don't know where, but far away in any case, another existence with somebody else awaited, but that I unwittingly interrupted that other life on that August night five years ago when, out of frivolity and laziness, I became Andrei's mistress.

I'll be completely honest and tell you that in such moments it's you I think of. I don't want to talk nonsense, and especially not now, after what happened last night, but why didn't I meet you six months before I did? Perhaps everything would have been different. Without your suspecting it, you have been perhaps the only thing I've been able to rely upon. I've enjoyed knowing you, apart from my affair with Andrei, apart from all we're involved in together, because, beyond the despair and comedy there, I knew that there was something else, a neutral space, an island of peace at the shores of which fear and suspicion and uncertainty fell away. I congratulated myself for not giving in to the temptation to speak to you and I was grateful to you for never asking me anything—precisely because in this way any confusion between my love for Andrei and my friendship with you was avoided and they remained two discrete domains. I hope you will believe me when I tell you that I never thought I would have to choose between them.

Why have you ruined a perfectly good arrangement? Now look how complicated things are getting, how confused! Yesterday I felt like a small catastrophe was unfolding and I wondered in panic if there was any escape. Still today, as I began writing to you, I was embarrassed and didn't really know what to tell you, afraid you'd misunderstand me or I'd express myself badly, and afraid above all that the path between us would always be blocked by this cruel accident, one so hard to see clearly and involving so many feelings that confuse me and pull me in contrary directions.

But now, having told you this, and through the act of telling, I've begun to see more clearly and I think I can say in all honesty that nothing has been lost: let's resume where we were before you disturbed everything yesterday and see what happens. We can do it. Listen to me, believe me, it can be done. Let me carry on with Andrei, with whom I have a past and an understanding and issues which can't be disposed of in a day or two or even a year. I've gone too far just to turn back, I'm too tired to reach the end. I think a love affair is such a complicated matter, such an exacting and sensitive mechanism, that I'm unable to extricate myself from its cogs alone, to cut the delicate ties that bind me, to break the siege of all the details which have grown out of it and now imprison me.

There are physical bonds between Andrei and me, similarities in how we see things, and though I may have lost the taste for or forgotten our common habits, I can't just break them, because at the very moment I do that they will make me suffer, just like an injured arm that gives you no trouble while you keep it still but will rack you with pain the moment you accidentally move it. I fear opening this old wound called love and feel that it is immeasurably better to leave my regrets and rebellions alone where they lie quietly today. Because, at least where I stand now, I'm an old friend of theirs and I feel at home with them in a way. The day I know that Andrei will never again ring my doorbell—that short, imperative sound that I could tell from a thousand others—I'll find myself disoriented once and for all. Understand this weakness and forgive me for it. Above all understand that nothing of what lies beyond that, what we share—our long conversations when you visit me for tea, our strolls through galleries, our disagreements about paintings and books, evenings at concerts, the way in public we can communicate with our eyes that we are in agreement about something that's happening—is of central importance in my life. And perhaps it's not central to yours either. But it's all that gives me back my self-respect and it's the only situation in which I'm able to see what Andrei's role in my life has been. He is the man who got the address wrong and knocked on the wrong door, an error which has lasted for five years and will last another five. But, in the end, it's a mistake I will live with. By which I mean, it's not one that I'm responsible for and need atone for.

You will come on Monday, won't you?

Arabela

ONE

turned down another offer today. I hope it's the last one. J. K. L. Wood, a correspondent and editor at the *New York Herald*, looked at me in frank amazement, ripped up the check that had been sitting on my desk for half an hour, and said drily, "Sir, you're no businessman." No, I'm not. But the idea of writing up a story in which I have a personal involvement for an illustrated magazine strikes me as ludicrous. I haven't been forgiven for robbing the music hall of a sensational act, Arabella and Partner, J. K. L. Wood has told me. We used to earn 620 dollars per show, plus travel expenses. The public wants to know how I could turn down such remuneration. It wants to know where Arabela is and—if possible—why Arabela loved me or why I loved her.

In the drawer on the right I have a photograph of her from our first summer together. It must have been in late August, in Talloires. (I should sort out my papers someday and date my photographs, where possible.) She's in a very light blue dress with an open white, flat collar, and wearing sandals, no socks, no hat, no face powder, but looking fresh and pale in the sunlight. The photograph catches her with her hand suddenly raised toward me—a nervous gesture in which she is not herself, because I think she wanted me to wait another moment before taking the picture. The thought of this little photograph appearing in a newspaper makes me shudder. It's not modesty or prejudice or sentimentalism, but I'm very private when it comes to certain things and the gesture captured in the picture is still startlingly immediate to me today.

⁂

It's astounding how the days when something remarkable happens in your life are pretty much the same as uneventful days—no signs or warnings. On that November evening I was to meet the press attaché of a friendly legation in place Pigalle to discuss some notes we had to edit together. He never showed. I couldn't face going home early. I walked up to Medrano. I love the smell of the circus ring, the violent red of the curtains at the back, from behind which you can hear the neighing of the horses awaiting their turn, the vulgarity of the female entertainers, the cavalryman-director's old-fashioned mustache, and the hearty, contagious laughter of the crowd. The pleasures of a disillusioned aesthete. But pleasures all the same.

It was well under way. It was silent as I entered. The silence, at a circus, that precedes potentially deadly acrobatics numbers. I glanced at the program.

TRIO DARTIES
Dikki et Miss Arabella

Two acrobats dressed in red, one on either side of the ring, were swinging on bars at great height, in synchronicity. In the center was a wooden bar, suspended from the ceiling by two ropes. In the ring, a kind of sleek-bald clown communicated what was about to happen with broad gestures. The acrobats in red had to fly through the air at the same time, from right and left respectively, to grasp the bar in the center with one arm simultaneously, and then each to swing onto the bar from whence the other had come. A double leap over a great distance at a height of about thirty meters, without a net.

The lights had gone down. Four spotlights, each a different color, shone up toward the acrobats. One light illuminated each person. A white spotlight shone on the empty bar between them, which gave its oscillations above the ring a sinister air. The fourth light was blue and shone weakly, higher up, and revealed the presence of another person, whom I had not noticed until that point—a woman, on a silk swing. She was dark, decked out in a silver maillot with a bracelet with big jewels on her right arm, and sat with her legs crossed, looking out with an attitude of utter indifference, the trace of a smile in the left corner of her mouth.

There was a sudden drumroll. Around me, nobody breathed. Then the steady pounding of a larger drum, and the acrobats flew through the air. Four arms grasped the central bar, it swung about once, and—it was all over. The bar again swung empty high above the ring and the two acrobats smiled, having swapped places, and the woman continued staring off into nothingness.

It was a mediocre number. That's what I thought then, with only my taste as a dilettante to go on. And that's my opinion still, after so many tours and much success. It was a mediocre number. Interesting, sure, and dangerous, but badly presented, with superfluous elements, and a fairground look and a theatrical style that I dislike. Later, in my peregrinations through the music halls of Europe, I learned that virtuosity and simplicity are two sides of the same coin. That's what Rastelli told me one evening in Hamburg, where we both happened to be performing; he with his balls, batons, and balloons, I with Arabela.

But I digress. The above passage should really be deleted. The stupid habits of a performer who can never stop thinking about his act and talking shop. So back to that November evening, when I was just the technical adviser to the Ministry of Health of Romania in its relations with the International Commission for Medical Cooperation. The number was over. The two gentlemen in red were standing in the middle of the ring, thanking the audience. A third man had appeared between them, also dressed in red, though he was younger and skinnier than them. I don't know where he'd been hiding up to that point. The bald clown described wide circles around them with a kind of grotesque, unamusing dance. While above us all the woman in the silk swing gazed out as though at the smoke of an imaginary cigarette. Almost imperceptibly, she flexed her feet like a ballerina at rest. She descended when the applause had ended, alternating arms as she gripped the rope in a slow, lazy motion downward, landing on her toes in the middle of the ring. Then she walked off, without haste and without a bow, between those two rows of servants in livery.

During the interval, as usual, I slipped off to look at the horses. They were grooming them for the show in open stalls in a gallery in the back. There was a smell of sand and manure and blood and perfume—a complex, deranged odor which I've only ever come across there and which I recall vividly. Elegant women wandered from stall to stall, caressing a black mane, wiping a foal's forehead clean, offering sugar bought at the door to a favorite horse.

In one corner, astride the wooden bar of a stall, the woman in the silver costume was talking to a black horse, a comradely arm over its neck. (I see a picture from one of those old greeting cards which they sent a long time ago, when I was a kid, for New Year's, with an Amazon and a horse gazing into each other's eyes beneath a horseshoe of flowers.) Later I learned that Miss Arabella wasn't there that evening because it gave her any pleasure; her contract required her to hang around in the interval in her show clothes, along with the conjurers and clowns, to flatter any spectators into thinking that they were witnessing behind-the-scenes action.

I wandered up to her casually. By which I mean, with no clear intention in mind. I offered her a cigarette. She accepted it, then remembered that smoking wasn't permitted there, and, as we'd ended up with unlit cigarettes in our mouths, she invited me back to her dressing room to smoke.

—Look, it's nearby. First door on the left.

I followed her, surprised at the ease with which she'd made the proposal. She talked to me as if we were old acquaintances, with a mix of indifference and friendliness, which is her natural manner in fact. But then—because we didn't know one another—I thought this manner was meant especially for me.

The second act of the show had begun, but was nothing remarkable, at least as far as the first few numbers were concerned, and the thought of chatting with this woman in a silver costume, in her role as a performer, appealed to me. It felt like a scene from a movie.

Still, I hesitated at the doorway. When she opened the door, I was startled to see that we weren't alone and that her three partners were already there, each in his own corner, gruff and immersed in the rigors of their toilet and ignoring us completely. I went in hesitantly, not sure if I should acknowledge them and put off, above all, by their hostile silence. They dressed slowly, morosely, without speaking, putting on shirts and trousers without prudishness. From time to time they'd send a towel or a comb or a shoehorn sailing over our heads. The only one to glance at me, looking up from the basin he was washing at, was the youngest one—the skinny boy who'd appeared at the end of the act.

—Beb, said the woman, addressing him.

Then she waved me over to her dressing table. She lit my cigarette, then lit hers from mine. She started to undo the buttons of her straps, but gave up so that she could smoke in peace and sat there with her back naked and one breast half-exposed beneath a top that wasn't quite loose enough to slip off her. I was surprised to see that she smoked awkwardly.

—Why do you hold the cigarette between your thumb and index finger?

—Don't know. I just do.

Neither of us spoke. I didn't know what to say and regretted having come. I was ridiculous among those three men, who carried on with their dressing as though I were invisible.

—Your number is very interesting, I finally said, limiting myself to this platitude, glad just to break the awkward silence.

—Interesting? I don't know. It's tiring. Isn't it, Beb? Tiring. She clasped her hands behind her neck and rocked her head between her arms. "And I don't even do anything.

I just watch from up there while they work. But the lights, that rickety apparatus, the laughter from the gallery...If you knew how stressful it all is..."

There was a note of deep weariness in her voice and she spoke with long pauses and watched the wraiths of smoke from her cigarette. But I was struck by the simplicity of those few words. Meanwhile, the men had finished dressing, and then something happened that was so unexpected that I think I would have burst out laughing had I not felt embarrassed. They lined up in front of Arabela, stopping with a certain bashfulness at about one pace from her. She looked at each of them in turn, inspecting their attire critically and making detailed observations.

—Change your collar tomorrow. I told you, never wear a collar for more than one day. And why aren't your boots polished? And why are you wearing your hat tilted back over your neck?

They took these criticisms like timid students, with the shy smiles of children who know they've done wrong and promise with their eyes to correct their mistakes. She dealt with the first two quickly (the two acrobats in red who'd performed the perilous leap). She ordered one to arrange the handkerchief in his pocket properly, as it was falling loose. She pointed out to the other that he had a vague stain on his lapel.

—I don't want to see that tomorrow!

She opened a drawer and took out a wad of money and divided it up. Each received his share with a submissive nod and left without counting it.

It was a little more complicated with Dikki, the bald clown, now a mere man with his face ruined with makeup, because Arabela spent more time getting his appearance in order. When, on receiving his cash, he asked for extra, Arabela replied severely:

—You'd better get moving! You have to be back early and no drinking, do you hear me? Beb, you stay! Look, your coat's missing a button.

The young man stood by the door while Arabela sewed a button on, gazing at him with a tenderness that struck me as comical in that place, and between two fully grown adults. All this was so unexpected that I could think of nothing to say when I was finally on my own with Arabela. I should have found the family scene I'd witnessed amusing, yet I found I was affected by it all: that young woman's tyrannical persona and the childlike docility of her comrades, their frightened respect for her, and the ironic, bossy way she dealt with them. She was younger than them—or possibly nearly their age—but she acted like an older sister and I couldn't reconcile her matronly demeanor with her tired adolescent expression.

—Don't you want to go back to the circus? she finally asked. "You shouldn't miss the equestrian number. It's good!"

I changed the subject with a sudden question.

—Do you like this life?

—What life?

—The one you're leading.

—You ask such questions...

She undid the laces of her white shoes and attended gravely to her stockings, dress, and powder as though to an important ceremony. She didn't ask me to look away or to turn off the light or to leave. She dressed in front of me with an utter lack of prudery, and yet there was something inexplicably chaste in the indifferent way in which she moved, something which prevented me from getting any ideas.

—If you like, I said, we could go somewhere nearby, for a drink and a talk.

—With pleasure, but it's a shame to miss a great show.

We went outside. It was raining lightly. A nighttime rain in which everything looks wet—the streetlights, the lights in the shop windows, and the walls of the houses suddenly ablaze in the headlights of a passing automobile. From afar, a café's friendly neon sign was flickering and I looked forward to the warmth and the hum of noise that awaited us there.

November evenings in Paris cafés, when you find yourself in front of empty bottles at midnight, choked by waves of smoke through which voices and dice and the clink of coins on the zinc bar are distant, shrouded, consoling sounds, and all part of a hubbub that tells you that you are after all not alone during these last days of autumn. How good it is to be among people you do not know who all become friends and confidants when gathered together in that evening hour among those foggy mirrors and the green felt of the billiard tables, as you look out at the street through windows sprinkled with raindrops that trace ephemeral maps and continents as the rivulets trickle down the glass. It's all familiar and anonymous in this neighborhood café, as on a train or a passenger ship, and the feeling that tomorrow you won't recognize any of the friendly faces around you somehow makes your defenses melt and makes you want to discuss your most private affairs with the stranger next to you. I listened to Arabela's story that evening, letting her tell it in her own way and in her own time, without interrupting her.

—A cabaret manager, a Swiss guy, one time put me in that swing you saw at the circus, somewhere near Montreux. He said he wouldn't hire the boys if I wasn't part of the act. 'But she can't do anything,' said Dik. 'Doesn't matter!' said the guy. 'Put her in there so people can see her—it doesn't work without a girl.' So that's what we did in the end and it stayed that way. I travel around with them, keep an eye on them, because they're all screwy and we have a show to do each evening. You've seen them. Dik drinks, Beb smokes, Jef chases women, and Sam can't be bothered about anything. (Funny names, but that's what I'm used to calling them and they always call me Arabela.) If I didn't keep them on a short leash…One of them is my brother, another my friend, the next I don't know what he is. Anyway, I'm used to them, and the setup works. Or maybe it doesn't, I don't know. Sometimes I just get so bored and I don't know what I'm doing up there on those ropes, where all I do is wait for our number to end…I don't usually smoke, but I'm not used to refusing an offer either—since I'm not used to getting any—so I accepted your cigarette. I hope you don't mind.

I let her talk for a long time. I don't remember now everything she told me. Ordinary things, occurrences, reflections, questions, memories—all in the same tired, offhand tone and without a flicker of light in her eyes, as though it were all equally unimportant. But she was probably tired, and I heard her out.

We left late. It was nearly two. The Métro stations had long since shut and there was no sign of a taxi. I suggested she come to my place.

—That's not possible.

—Of course it is. I'm inviting you to sleep, not for anything else. It's closer and simpler.

She thought about it for a moment and it was clear she wasn't hesitating out of prudery, but was calculating whether it was more comfortable to go with me or not. In the end she agreed it was simpler.

—I'll come.

We went up to the third floor of a nearby lodging house where I was living. There was only one bed so I told her I'd take the armchair in the next room. I meant it in good faith.

—No, she replied. You'll sleep in the bed. It's big enough for both of us and I suppose we'll manage.

I accepted, because it made no difference and it wasn't the first time I'd slept next to a woman with nothing else implied. Various friends, male and female, would often end up at my place after a party and sleep wherever they could make do. But when I turned off the light and sank into the familiar warmth of the pillows, the slow breathing of the woman next to me, her heart burdened with some private sorrow, felt so close and familiar, and I could feel her body throbbing so close beside me. To the dull sound of the rain still falling in the street, I took her arms and put them around my neck, happy that she was next to me. She submitted to me without any reproach for having broken my word, but at the same time passively, absurdly, calmly, and without enthusiasm. She tasted of warm bread and that feeling I still have inside is the only sure thing I have left of Arabela, today, after so many years living together and so many of separation.

When our embrace ended she turned over, facing the window, said she was very tired, and fell instantly into a deep sleep.

TWO

've never tried to explain to anybody how Arabela ended up with me and how I, always so steadfast in defending my freedom, entered into such a serious relationship. It all happened so simply and impetuously that I'm sure any explanation would be false. Arabela stayed out of laziness, just as she came.

—How about staying here and abandoning the tour? I suggested, the next day.

—Dunno. Let's give it a try.

And by evening she'd moved in. She'd brought a small suitcase and a few toiletries—her entire baggage. I asked her how she'd settled things with her colleagues.

—They've gone away.

—Was it tough?

—No. I explained things to them and they left. I didn't do anything anyway.

The situation should have been awkward, with this woman whom I'd met only the day before and who had, on the basis of a few casual words, given up a life, or a career at least, to throw her lot in with a strange man with whom she had nothing in common. But how can I explain that feeling of calm I had from the very first, the familiar atmosphere Arabela brought to my room, the tone of shared memories created by the sound of her footsteps through our home? She knew how to open precisely the drawer she needed, to find where things were located, to turn on the light without asking me where the switch was, to put a book back in its place. She found everything on her own, instinctively. By intuition, I suppose.

We went out for dinner, then to a local cinema, and got home late, not in any rush—at least not on my part—because although I liked the warmth of her arm and I was looking forward to having her entirely naked beside me, in bed, she felt so familiar beside me that it all savored of an old love affair and a settled passion, as though we had been together for years and were used to each other's physical presence.

I've always been an oddball and a loner, always protected my freedom any time a woman tried to tie me down. I'm a bachelor by nature and I hadn't understood until then how living with someone could be possible. I, who always lived for surprise and temporary arrangements, found the idea of coming across the same body with the same reactions every night absurd. Perhaps I could find some way to explain how Arabela made me abandon my vocation as a vagabond in love from our first moment together, but why bother using psychology to explain something that happened so naturally and which I welcomed gladly? No, no, Arabela would laugh if she read such a thing. All I remember is that she smelled lovely. She had a faint aroma of perfume, warmed by her blood; a slightly animal smell, redolent of night. It was incredible how her skin transformed a banal and inexpressive cologne into such an alluring aroma that she seemed to exhale it.

—*Que tu sens bon!* I told her sincerely, when I wanted to tell her how much I loved her, and I would find it very hard to translate that into Romanian. I think it would sound ridiculous.

In the evening, when I got home from work, the memory of that smell would hit me from afar, filling my mouth and nose like the warm aroma of roasted chestnuts, and I'd take those stairs with the impatience of an adolescent, to get home and to embrace her and press my cheek to hers.

There haven't been many women in my life. But there have been a few. As many as any man of average unattractiveness might have, when he acts kindly and knows when to insist. I'm not boasting, as I know any number of acquaintances of mine, taller and darker and better-looking, who have had ten times the number of "conquests." Still, I've never met a woman—and I've been in love with some of them—who has ever given me the sense of cool sensuality that I found in Arabela's arms, as I inhaled the smell of her warm, lazy, indifferent flesh.

Because Arabela wasn't a passionate woman, and it wasn't an affair of passion. When I got into what they call my "mess"—when the ministry back home informed me I was suspended from duty—I know that my well-wishing friends back in Bucharest were alarmed and told me they pitied me, and spread the news that I'd fallen into the clutches of a femme fatale. I laughed, looking at that femme fatale in her housedress, almost always of a rough, warm color, doing chores about the room like a real house-wife or fetching a book for me that I'd mislaid. There was something so conjugal and maternal about her (her seri-ous, domineering expression in the evening when she took care of me, just as she'd taken care of Beb and Dik before), that the idea that someone could mistake Arabela for the somber heroine of a novel cracked me up.

—What's wrong with you, Stefan? Why are you laughing?

—Nothing, sweetheart! I like watching you...

—You're not in your right mind.

No, I was not in my right mind at all. On the day I completed my preliminary study for the international com-mission, to which I had been sent as a medical adviser to the Ministry of Health, I should have returned home nicely to Romania and submitted my report. That's really what I should have done. That's what Arabela advised me to do. I couldn't. I'm not saying that I'd have been devastated with-out her or claiming I couldn't have managed. I don't think splitting up would have been terribly difficult. It was nothing like that. Still, I didn't leave. Giving up her closeness and her full body—a little too full, to tell the truth, but so warm and welcoming—and forgetting those calm arms which I caressed with my lips evening after evening, from her shoulder down to her wrists and hands, seemed a bit too much of an effort. And on the other hand, I couldn't take her back with me to my country, for many reasons (including, I must admit, a degree of cowardice; it would have been difficult to turn up in Bucharest with Arabela, where a number of respectable friends were expecting me, including a woman—Maria—whom I'd been pointlessly in love with for a long time and whose regard I still craved, precisely because we'd taken great pains never to allow ourselves to be more than close friends).

To leave there—how dull! I just stayed, and there was nothing heroic about my decision. Just as back in my high school days when I'd sometimes wake at dawn and look at the clock in panic, then, after a brief hesitation, pull the quilt over my head, happily resolving to skip school.

I didn't go to school, even at dawn on those January mornings when my diplomatic case was expected in Bucharest and when, looking out the wide windows of our room at a long strip of overcast Parisian sky, I told Arabela I was staying. Sanctions soon followed. First a warning for grave dereliction of duty. Then my suspension. If I wasn't prosecuted and punished more severely it was because Andrei

Giorgian, a friend and political dilettante who had since become a member of Parliament for Turda and then a very serious undersecretary of foreign affairs, had apparently put a good word in for me. Andrei wrote to me in a personal capacity also (I recall it was printed on official ministerial stationery, which amused me greatly) and told me off for my frivolity. In the postscript he informed me that he was going to marry Maria (whom he had in any case been living with for some time, this being the same Maria to whom, at a ball one evening some years before, I had made an inappropriate confession, which I regret still). The postscript in itself made no sense to me, as their wedding had been announced in the papers and I'd already written to congratulate them.

I took all this friendly advice and criticism with equanimity. Not because I was looking to annoy anybody or to quarrel. No. Just because there was nothing I could say, and because there was no way I could talk about Arabela and about the gentle happiness I had found in loving her and about the deep, orderly, simple voluptuousness of my nights in the rue Tholoze. It was funny to think that in everybody else's eyes I had fallen prey to this dark girl who, even in her most heightened moments of passion, was unable to smile any differently from how she'd smiled up there on her silk swing, detached and weary.

THREE

hings went well while the money lasted. For about four months. I began with nearly thirty thousand francs in my account from the good times. Enough that I didn't start out worrying unduly. In the meantime, we had enough to live on—and that was all I cared about, though I was no bohemian by nature.

I can remember almost nothing of the first months of my love for Arabela. I see her quiet, steady, and house-proud, leaving me free to wander where I wished during the day and docile when I got back home. She'd take my arm and nestle against me when we went out, and stretch out in the bed at night like a pale, purring cat when it was very cold outside and very warm inside and I went to kiss her. I forgot I had a career, forgot I had to work, and turned back into the chaotic first-year student who'd missed anatomy lectures to attend concerts at the Colonne. This time around, I found another pastime: I spent the mornings in the Louvre and the afternoons reading Vasari's *Lives of the Artists* in the National Library, always in the same armchair—118—and under the same green-tinted lamp.

I was grateful to Arabela for unintentionally knocking me off my reasonable, predestined course and turning the serious gentleman she'd met that November night into somebody who forgot that he was a doctor, adviser, and diplomat and became again what he had always wanted to be: a young man.

When summer came we went to Talloires and stayed in a guesthouse that was very cheap but had a fashionable veneer (which flattered Arabela's bourgeois tastes), and cheerfully played the role of happy young couple in the society of friendly, gossipy people. Arabela shone with pride among her friends at the guesthouse, who were all decent wives. How well the air of married woman became her, having spent so many years playing the role of perpetual fiancée in a shady, unstable carnival world. I was truly pleased that I had given Arabela the one deep pleasure to which she was fitted: the illusion of legitimate love. And I enjoyed seeing her slowly lose the shade of suspicion, or perhaps panic, which in the past had sometimes clouded her smile.

Those idyllic months came to a brutal end when we returned to Paris and I calculated that I had six thousand francs left.

—I have to do something, I told Arabela, with an embarrassed shrug.

—*We* have to do something, she corrected me.

When I came home in the evening I found her in good spirits, considering the mess things were in, anyway. She was very brave and was clear about what we had to do.

—Listen, Stefan, six thousand francs is a lot of money. You can't appreciate that. It can last us five months at least. The doorman's just told me maybe there's an apartment free from the fifteenth. We can move to another neighborhood, preferably on the Left Bank, toward the Porte d'Orléans or the Porte de Versailles. You can get cheap rooms there for a hundred and fifty or two hundred francs and we're sure to get a good one even if it's on an upper floor. We can eat at home in the evening, I'll take care of that. Lunch—there are clean little places, you'll see! We'll stay at home mostly and when we do go out, well, I think there's a second class on the Métro—isn't there?

—For forty-five centimes!

—You've no right to talk that way. You've no idea what forty-five centimes means. Oh, and don't forget: try smoking Gauloises; they're cheaper and taste better.

—Poverty, in other words, I reflected with an exaggerated sigh, to hide the real worry I felt.

—Not poverty! Certainty! For five months only, but certainty in any case. After that...well, we'll see what happens.

Arabela had turned back into the authoritative, exacting woman I had seen on the first evening in her dressing room at the Medrano, inspecting her partners and giving them brief orders which they then meekly obeyed.

Ten days later we'd moved. Arabela had taken care of everything—the negotiations, the deposit, quarrels, and boredom—while I, after panicking for a few days ("What do we have to do? What's going to happen?"), resumed my methodical wandering through the neighborhoods of Paris, with occasional stops in art galleries and bookstores, returning home exhausted in the evening, but with the unutterably calm feeling that there was someone who on my behalf was thinking through the "problems of life"— as Arabela gravely called them whenever we happened to have a serious discussion. Our new residence was a small room on the sixth and top floor of a row of houses with black walls and scabrous plasterwork, in an immense yard where weeds grew freely and there were many children. Somewhere in the vicinity of the Porte de Versailles. I don't know if a day passed when I didn't see laundry hung out to dry from a window for a nonexistent sun, as it never poked its way into the yard. At the same time every day you could hear old records being played on a phonograph—a hoarse, unremitting voice. I don't know what floor it issued from as I could never locate the source. A complicated staircase led up to our apartment and I'd stop about five times, in front of various doors, and read those same bohemian name cards: ALEXANDRE MERENSKI, *artiste-peintre*; THEODOR VAN HAAS, *tenor*; MARCEL CHARDE, *paysagiste*...Only painters, poets, and singers—a poverty-stricken demimonde in which I felt out of place. I, who had never had anything to do with the arts and who, apart from a minor interest in books, did not feel its pull.

And yet... I'd forget the neighborhood and my neighbors, the stained walls of the house, the yard festooned with damp long johns flapping in the breeze, the windows, the stairwell with its damp wallpaper and artistic name cards—forget it all, as soon as I opened the door and entered our sixth-floor room which Arabela, with her genius as a homemaker, had rendered tidy and tasteful and harmonious, from the polished wooden furniture to the cold winter flowers that were never absent from our table, even on days when we had no money for bread! I should laugh when I remember the honest-to-goodness beauty of that room, presided over by the white apron Arabela wore with a hint of pride—but if I don't laugh it's primarily because I've always lacked taste and secondly because I left something in that room which is not to be laughed at.

We were soon well-known in the neighborhood. Arabela first made it her business to know the storekeepers, aware that hard times could lie ahead. She cultivated them with charm and determination. She was well in with the saleswoman at the Maggi dairy store on the corner, exchanged friendly greetings with the butcher, asked after the baker's children, who were always sick and with whom Arabela shared her knowledge of various home remedies. As a result of these useful connections, we went up in the estimation of our neighbors, and I remember how Arabela was almost proud when one day, a week before it happened, the baker confided that the price of a loaf was going to drop from 2.40 to 2.35. I can't recall if I was flattered also by this, but it gave us a certain local standing.

When we crossed the place Vaugirard on our way home, usually arm in arm, either because we were in love or from the cold, our acquaintances would smile at us from their respective stores and more than once I heard the whisper behind us, *Voilà la jeune ménage du sixième qui passe.* I didn't dislike this description of us, and the respectability it conferred to our arrangement made Arabela truly happy.

We'd stop on the way to buy our groceries for the evening meal and every time I'd admire her ability to turn a tight budget and limited ingredients into a new and surprising dish. I've tried many times since to improvise a similar feat and never succeeded, which—silly as it sounds—makes me despair. I find myself thinking of Paris sometimes and dreaming of going back and seeing those streets that I love so much as if they are people, but I have to make the ridiculous admission that the first thing I'd like to do on returning there is to go into a charcuterie and spend one franc twenty-five centimes on a quarter kilo of *céleri rémoulade*. I've given the recipe to all my hosts here in Romania but on every occasion the celeriac in mustard sauce that's served up bears no resemblance to the piquant, flavorsome, engaging *céleri rémoulade* which graced our dinners in a little room on the sixth floor of a building on the rue d'Alésia, under the eyes of Arabela, who gladly indulged our appetites, especially such inexpensive and innocent ones.

She, who to my knowledge was utterly lacking in vanity, and back at the circus would respond to compliments with a tired shrug, and later, when she'd achieved glory, responded to critical acclaim with a confused smile, would redden and be absurdly proud when I said I liked something she'd cooked or told her a sauce was good. She loved me doubly and when we went to bed I could feel her even more tender and grateful than I knew her to be usually, as a young, healthy, undemonstrative girl. They were her private pleasures as the woman of that poor household. A household we could barely keep together on the last of those dwindling savings, despite our scrimping and saving. I'd left the housekeeping to Arabela and had nothing in my pockets but the pennies she gave me for cigarettes and even when I happened to get hold of some money—a loan, or by selling a book or pawning a watch—I handed it all over to her, and she gritted her teeth and dealt with the poverty and the debts to shopkeepers who were becoming ever harder to reckon with.

The hardest thing was not being able to pay the rent. I can manage a certain nostalgia for the days without enough to eat, and walking to save on buses, and worn-out clothes, but the memory of not having 175 francs to give to the landlord for a month's rent still makes me shudder with fear, and it's something I wish I could forget. Those winter mornings when we slipped quietly down the stairs so that nobody would catch us escaping! And late at night, when we walked about outside, avoiding going home until after midnight, when the light went out in the concierge's office, so that we could creep back up the six flights of stairs, close to the wall, holding our breath—one more to go, just one—trembling for fear that at any moment somebody could shout out and stop us on the road to our salvation. Our salvation was the door at the top of the stairs, which we closed behind us with a sigh of relief, double-locking it and leaning against it as though it were a fortress we'd struggled to take.

Then we would sink into a long night filled with forgetfulness and peace, wishing it would never end, holding each other in a long embrace that we took in voluptuous stages, from kiss until release, until sleep delivered us from the exhaustion caused by poverty and love. Arabela's head would fall heavily on my shoulder. In the dark I liked to look at her hair, shining like wet coal.

FOUR

t was still midwinter and the moment had come when we really had to figure out what we were going to do. I was nervous and ineffectual, Arabela was calm and practical.

—I may be back late this evening, she said one day. Wait for me in the square, across the road from the post office, between six and seven. We'll see what happens...

What she came back with that evening was an offer for a paltry, dubious opening in an acrobatics act in a cabaret theater on the periphery of the city. Twenty-two francs per evening.

—All right Arabela, so you want to go back to that?

—I don't want to go back to anything. Particularly not to "that." I want for us to be able to pay the rent.

She went back to "that" without disgust or complaint, with the simple knowledge that she had to work to earn some money. She had no doubts or hesitation.

—What else can we do?

She invoked the same simple logic a month later when she asked me to come to the theater to accompany her in a duet.

There are abominable things like this which become absolutely natural when referred to in a simple tone such as that which Arabela used. Though you realize the enormity of what was being asked, you go along with it.

—You see, next week the program is changing. I finish up with the acrobatics and start with dancing. An Apache dance. I need an accordionist and I think you play the piano.

I accepted. If I had to explain to someone I knew why I accepted, I'd only talk nonsense and I'm sure they wouldn't understand a thing. I accepted, that's all.

Oh, the evenings at Montrouge, at that cabaret—half theater, half dance hall—where I accompanied Arabela on an off-key accordion. Her dance was comically amateurish (she'd never been a dancer) and yet attained elegance through her body's natural ability to respond beautifully to melody! Outside was that other life that I'd fled precipitously, and to which I could always return, with a little effort—but the feeling of having thrown it all away of my own free will made me love my fate tenfold, among those tables of eager consumers and their long glasses with mint-green drinks. No doubt about it, I liked my new career and sometimes when I was doing well and I was asked to repeat a song, and every drinker in the place joined in, I felt a little shiver of pride, which announced that the performer in me was coming out.

From there we moved on to local movie theaters and musette dances, adapting our act to each show, with me presenting Arabela's light acrobatics act one day and accompanying her dance routine on the piano the next, and sometimes, if necessary, taking a few steps with her when her dance required a partner.

The timing was perfect for us, in that year when the main-street movie theaters were showing their first talking pictures and the local silent-movie theaters, alarmed at the competition from this innovation, were trying to keep their audiences with "extra attractions" (as the posters described them). In those days you came across a lot of "snake-men," "mermaids," "magicians," and acrobats and imitators, among whom we found a niche, as demand was high and the programs were always changing, which forced us to make epic tours of the gates of Paris, from quarter to quarter, but without ever leaving an area that stretched from Denfert-Rochereau in the south to Batignolles in the north. I thought we'd never escape the borders of that suburban world and break into the center of Paris, where the names of the theaters were written in lights and where the colored billboards shone inaccessibly in the distance. But I very soon got to know a young pederast poet with connections in the world of nighttime entertainment. The young fellow had seen Arabela dancing and was fired up about her art and swore he'd get her a shot. Sure, he was a flake, and throughout all this I was skeptical about the value of my love's dancing and took these promises of glory with a pinch of salt. And yet it was all thanks to him that we got a place in the program at the Bobino, the famous Montparnasse cabaret, and so danced there with Arabela for two weeks, right on the rue de la Gaîté. True, none of the critics ever remarked us, but we earned the fabulous sum of hundreds of francs.

Naturally, we moved out of the sixth-floor garret, but we stayed in that quarter, which in a way we'd now become dependent on. Arabela, because of the good relationships she'd built up there, I for the color of the place and because of the harmonious background noise of neighborhood sounds that I now felt so at home with that I couldn't have thought or read better than I did in that sea of sounds—the rumbling and clattering of a store's shutters going up, a factory whistle, the fading melody played on a harmonica, or raucous swearing from the street where a couple of drivers were coming to blows.

Place de la Convention! Some nights, when I had trouble sleeping, I imagined wandering with my hands in my pockets and my overcoat unbuttoned through that square, toward the Porte de Versailles and heading slowly up, first taking the sidewalk on the right, then the sidewalk on the left, stopping attentively before every storefront to revisit every detail; the name of the store, the window with its display of goods, whether cheap or sumptuous, and the fogged glass...The smell of boiled potatoes, raw meat, bananas...A cornucopia of goods was scattered around me: calico, fish, oranges, buttons and braces, butter, eggs, and tinned goods. And voices ringing in the air and lights shining from one side of the street to the other...I see again the familiar faces of the people there; the smiling old lady in the lobby of the Hotel Messidor, the young woman selling artichokes on the corner of rue Blomet, the glassware vendor on the other side of the road who looked like Napoleon III and who, because the number 10 bus stopped outside his store, had adopted the manner of a stationmaster...And I see Arabela coming down from the rue de Croix-Nivert, where we lived, in her rain jacket, hurrying through the passersby only to stop at length at the entrance to a store to buy a spool of thread, looking with childlike wonder at the big display windows and calculating how much money she had in her pocket, then moving on and buying a bottle of wine from the Primistère, where they handed out the prize coupons she collected assiduously in the hope of one day winning the "twelve-person" table set displayed in the photograph in the window. And not only in the hard times, struggling with unpaid rent and the last of our bus tickets, but later too, when we'd earned a bit of money and made a pleasant home of our new apartment in Croix-Nivert. Arabela stubbornly refused to accommodate herself to our new situation as artists who had played the Bobino and as a result of the show had come to know many people from "good society" who came to see us perform.

She still wanted to be a housewife, sometimes ostenta-
tiously exaggerating her domestic chores.

Hard to define what kind of people our new friends were.
One was some kind of a painter, another some kind of a poet,
another some kind of a critic, and so on—all of them young
and disillusioned, drawn from late-night Montparnasse cafés.
Some were homosexuals, others just snobs (as far as debauch-
ery and exhibitionism were concerned). Others, the great
minority, were decent fellows, but lazy, and in the meantime
unemployed. I couldn't really figure out what their situation
was, though almost all of them painted, wrote, or acted, and
some of them made a point of mentioning their literary connections (going so far as showing me a signed letter from
Cocteau) or their successes in the distant past—which they'd
prove by pulling out an old poster or a few lines of praise in
Nouvelles Littéraires. I enjoyed the color and liveliness they
brought to our two rooms, which otherwise would have been
dominated by Arabela's gentle, slow temperament, which
was like an ember buried in ashes. I have no idea if any of
them had any talent or artistic vocation. Perhaps they had!
I'm not competent to judge that kind of thing, but I wouldn't
be surprised if one or two of them have since achieved something, and if I were to pick up one of the foreign newspapers
today to find good news written there about them.

There was a vague whiff of rebellion about us, as it was
undoubtedly revolutionary of them to despise the produc-
tions at the opera and to admire instead a dancer of popular

numbers from the suburbs. Hadn't one of them written in
one of those avant-garde publications—one of those incen-
diary publications read by exactly seventeen people, each
ready to turn the world upside down—that everything
Wagner had written should be burned and that Bruno
Walter (who was directing *Die Meistersinger von Nürnberg*
at the Opéra at the time) should be thrown out, in order
for Wagner's place to be taken by my darling Arabela? The
same Arabela who couldn't stand any of them, because she
only liked decent, orderly people and utterly detested anything adventurous, bohemian, or "artistic." This girl, who
had come from the world of the circus, after an unsettled
childhood and endless wandering from town to town, this
girl who was more easy than virtuous, having surrendered
to me at any rate on the first night, without my pressing her,
had a bourgeois aversion for all that wasn't legitimate and
clean. She suffered in the company of the pederasts and les-
bians who abounded around the bars where we played and
was horrified by the morals of our recent friends, among
whom she passed with a chaste, judgmental frown.

One evening, after a long dinner of mussels and white
wine in the studio of a young painter, where we happened
to meet a group of crazy girls and drunken boys, I was hus-
tled off in a friend's car to the Bois de Boulogne, to attend a
partouza. Arabela and I had heard this word used but neither
of us had more than a vague idea what it meant, other than
that it involved certain sexual rites with groups of people

and that it occurred among the darkest laneways in the Bois. The experience began mysteriously, with the automobiles signaling back and forth to each other by flicking their headlights on and off a number of times. It was explained to us that this was how the initiates communicated their presence to each other. A long line of limousines rode forward with their headlights off toward the center of the woods, and from time to time two or three separated from the group. After the necessary signaling, they would turn off to the right or left together. It seemed that the basic condition for a successful *partouza* was for the partners not to know one another: the men swapped places, going from one automobile to the other, thereby swapping women also. They loved in the dark, with the lights out and curtains drawn, without any preliminaries, without being seen, almost without speaking, spurred on by the cheap mystery of darkness and anonymity.

Up to that point the matter seemed mythical to me. But now I had before me this mysterious procession of vehicles, observed the signaling of the headlights through the passenger window, saw the shapes of those who had reached an understanding slipping through the darkness. My curiosity was so aroused by the intensity of the spectacle, I admit, that it blocked out any trace of moral reserve I might have possessed. No, it wasn't disgusting. It was thrilling. You would have needed Arabela's lack of imagination and her fundamental sincerity to have been revolted there in the name of decency. She gripped my arm and shouted that she wouldn't have anything to do with such filth (yes, she said "filth," to my shame and to the embarrassment of the people of taste in our company). In the meantime, however, our friends had spotted a blue limousine and were hurrying after it, to get away from that busy laneway and to find a more suitable place for the first advances. I was taking part in the journey with genuine excitement, astounded by the simplicity of the escapade and waiting with bated breath to see how it would all turn out—but Arabela wouldn't settle down. She thrashed about in my arms, screaming that she wanted to go home and threatening to smash the windows if we didn't stop.

—You're pigs, you hear? Pigs! And you, you're the same as the rest of them. Why won't you stop? I want you to stop! You bandits! I'll report you to the police. Give me a pencil to put down their number. I said, give me a pencil!

She took an envelope from her purse and, because she didn't have a pencil, took used lipstick to record the number of the automobile hurtling ahead of us. Her hand trembled as she formed the five figures in thick, bright-red, childish strokes. There was something about this panicked gesture that only increased the tension of our adventure and made me feel as though I were in a detective story.

A long, panicked screech sounded from somewhere in front of us. A screech and a shout, perhaps. We jolted to a halt. A moment of tense silence ensued. Nobody moved. Everybody listened for another sound to come through the darkness. It was like a train stopping unexpectedly at night on a bridge in the middle of the countryside. Nobody knew what had happened or dared to guess. A collision? A catastrophe? A threat? All that could be heard was the distant mechanical panting of the locomotive...

Then human figures and voices could be made out around us. Men were running ahead to see what had happened. Beyond the shut automobile doors, the alarmed whispering of a woman could be heard. I got out. A gentle rain was falling. In the distance was a cluster of agitated lights. Arabela stepped out also and walked wordlessly alongside. We made our way past parked automobiles and could hear the long sighs of impassioned embraces which the panic had not interrupted. The cold air of that March night had an unbearable smell of intimacy, perfume, and blood—I found it hard to tell them apart.

About a hundred paces away, a large ring of people had formed. We approached, apprehensively. There had been an accident. We intuited this from the whispers of the people gathered there and from the respectful distance they kept from what they were looking at. Only when I was very close did I see that it was a wounded person. They all stared at him from a distance, intimidated, not daring to approach. It was a boy of about sixteen who had been passing through on a bicycle and had been crushed by an automobile moving at speed with its headlights off.

Arabela pushed her way through the people and went forward, alone among them. A lock of her black hair had fallen over her forehead and she didn't bother to brush it aside, so intent was she. She kneeled beside the injured boy and gazed at him unflinchingly. Then she rolled up her sleeves, looked for a clean handkerchief and asked for some water. Somebody hurried to bring her some. I don't know from where; perhaps from the carburetor of one of the automobiles. She lifted the wounded boy's head and laid it in her lap. The headlights showed a cracked skull and a clump of bloody hair. A woman next to me wearing an elegant dress began to scream hysterically. It was clear from her flushed cheeks and heavy breathing that the accident had interrupted her moment of passion. Arabela stared her down—a gaze I don't think I could have met, had it been directed at me.

There was nothing to be done. It had been obvious from the first moment that the boy lying there on the wet earth was dead. I could tell that much, from whatever remained of my old medical knowledge. Meanwhile, the police arrived. I took Arabela by the arm and pulled her away from there. We walked for a long time in silence, grateful for the sound of the rain pattering around us, helping us not to think about anything, and particularly not about ourselves. Finally, we came upon a stray taxi, and it brought us home in half an hour. During the ride, Arabela sat completely still, unreachable. As soon as we were home she threw herself down on the bed, fully clothed, and wept with abandon, like a child, her body racked with sobbing. It was all that could be done to redeem that night.

FIVE

e never discussed what had happened. For several days, we tiptoed around one another and spoke little, trying to keep busy to avoid looking one another in the eye. In the end, we forgot about it. Looking back today, Arabela's violent reaction that evening, her fear and her disgust at perversion and death, which turned several days later into a weary smile, now strikes me, on reflection, as less silly than it did at the time. I didn't understand then the strange halo she seemed to wear. It's hard to understand some things when you're too close to them.

And still, these qualities were probably expressions of what critics would later refer to as her "genius." So many articles have been written about Arabela, about her art, about her moving stage presence—and none of them get to the heart of it. I myself, accompanying her on the piano with all my attention, yet startled by the charm of her voice, was intrigued by the mystery of that feeling. It was like the mystery of a plaything you'd invented but which slips from your hands and the limits of your understanding. Who could have foretold, that day when we were offered the chance to perform a set of *chansonettes* in that little provincial cabaret-theater, where our little adventure would lead? Not I, in any case, because it was a ridiculous proposal.

—A hundred and sixty francs per evening, said Arabela, isn't an offer you get every day.

—It certainly isn't. But you're an acrobat, or a dancer at a stretch, so I can't see how you're going to sing, dear girl, even for a hundred times that sum.

She laughed, astounded by my reasoning. Hers was more straightforward. We'd been offered a chance to sing in a provincial cabaret. To sing, not to dance. So we'd sing.

—Darling, she said, I've spent my whole life doing what's been asked of me. Nobody has ever asked what I want, what I know how to do, what I'm able to do. So I've never taken the time to tell anybody. You say this offer we've got is a mistake. Maybe so. But it's still a contract and it's not to be spurned, it's to be signed.

It wasn't my first time yielding to Arabela and adventure. Several days later our act was ready. We rehearsed frantically—me at the piano, Arabela while doing housework—several fashionable songs, a couple of classic melodies, and, as a crowd-pleaser, an old ballad from Auvergne, the region where we'd be performing. We'd got the ballad from the musical friends of Monsieur Pierre, the owner of the glassware store, and an excellent baritone and a clarinet player in the arrondissement's brass band. I found Arabela's voice pleasant, but nothing more, and I certainly didn't anticipate the dizzy, overwhelming success that would keep us at that theater for a month, followed by some big cities in the Midi, opulent seaside towns and old-style holiday resorts.

They were glorious evenings, with perhaps excessively warm enthusiasm from the audience. They encouraged us boisterously, as though at a match, but there were also charged moments of silence, with the whole room holding its breath at the last note of that ballad from the Auvergne, as Arabela drew it out like a thread of silk, passing the gleaming thread between her fingertips. That was when I felt that note of personal sadness suspended in Arabela's song, struggling out despite her limitations and her attitude and bearing as an "artist." The deep seam of feeling I was mining was beyond my comprehension, but I decided to try to simplify our act and to create a set that was more coherent than that grab bag of melodies we'd started with.

Those who later heard Arabela in Paris that evening at the Empire, now famous in the annals of the music hall, will never know the metamorphoses through which our act passed before becoming that perfect incarnation later popularized in the illustrated magazines. Everything was hard won, day after day, through numerous modifications: from Arabela's dress to her sleek, straight-cut hair, the black curtains that framed us, the way I sat at the piano, the order of the songs in the set, the silver bracelet on Arabela's left wrist, and the way she let her long arms hang lazily at her sides, with her hands clasped about her knees. And, if I forced myself, perhaps I could still recall today when and where each detail in our music hall act emerged, whether in Brest or in Nîmes, as we refined our stage presence and décor with each new appearance in each new town.

The hardest thing was how to position Arabela onstage. Though she was calm and absolutely immune to stage fright, she was completely unable to find a natural pose while she sang. She didn't know what to do with her hands or how to move or what to lean on. We tried everything. Standing next to me at the piano, as though reading the music over my shoulder. Up at the front of the stage, on the right, leaning against a small podium. And finally, on the right, leaning slightly over the rear of the piano. Nothing worked, until one glorious day, when we were rehearsing, I yelled at her in exasperation and told her to get onto the piano. She seated herself very comfortably, as though on an armchair, and she immediately recovered her self-confidence. Settled there, with her legs crossed and her hands clasped over her knee, it was as though she were sitting again on that silk swing in her old circus days. And that melancholy, indifferent smile that illuminated her from within came back—the one from the evening we first met.

No, I don't know the source of that current of feeling in her voice or the stark yet sometimes mysterious beauty of her singing. I sometimes still listen today to the gramophone records we made then (fortunately they are few and hard to find) and I wonder why I don't have the key to their mystery, even though I participated in it and it took place before my very eyes. She had a weak, flat voice, slightly off-key, but from the moment she opened her mouth it was as though she were drawing back heavy curtains and opening a doorway to a world of dreams. Her singing was spirited but awkward at the same time, like a beginner who has mastered a melody on the piano and is herself surprised to hear a note of hesitation later on, after success should have allowed a sense of confidence. But she sang without verve and without any appealing gestures or smiles. She always sang—whether it was a ballad or something lyrical—in that same even, diligent tone, like a sad child.

I don't think she was ever theatrical or even had moments of pride. She believed the job she was doing was no better or worse than any other, and I'm sure that if she'd had to sew or embroider she would have applied herself with the same degree of conscientiousness. Her attitude of honesty and decency had nothing to do with "art," and if Arabela's singing was indeed moving it was not due to her technical ability or her modest voice. It was due to the weariness of her soul, the depth of her melancholy, and the dim light which suffused her life, circumstances, and memories.

One day, before our return to Paris and our debut at the Empire, I recalled a vacation I'd spent a long time before, in my student days, in a village in the Alps, where I had met and loved a young girl for one night. The girl then disappeared utterly from my life. Remembering those days, I asked Arabela to sing me some verses from a song from a game from that time.

Il court, il court le furet,
Le furet du bois joli,
Il a passé par ici,
Le furet du bois, Mesdames,
Il repassera par là . . .

I didn't know that in asking her to do this I'd accidentally stumbled across the most beautiful song in our repertoire, the one to which we would very soon owe our fame, the melody that would go around the metropolises of Europe for a whole year and be played on gramophones, on the radio, in jazz clubs, by Viennese orchestras, and be whistled at night in deserted streets by people who'd stayed out too late. The song was astounding from the first for its simplicity (it was daring to perform a song children sang in the playground on the stage of a prestigious theater), but it was its very ingenuousness that must have made it appealing and created a crowd of imitations. It was the revival of the waltz, of the songs of 1900, the paintings of Toulouse-Lautrec and Vuillard, of long dresses and three-pointed hats, all in one and reduced to the tastes of the moment, with a certain sweet nostalgia for those happy years before the war.

The only personal credit I can claim for our lucky, glorious career is for intuiting the poetic potential of a set of old-fashioned songs. While our friends urged us to perform modern music and Arabela was tempted to do one of the new songs, I insisted we limit ourselves to outmoded melodies from between 1900 and 1920, knowing that a decade-old song, when revived, has the advantage over a new one of being able to infuse all our little feelings about the past with nostalgia and lightness.

So, from the amnesia of the fashionable generations, I saved an entire repertoire of songs that had been wept to and danced to at another time, and made them contemporary. There was no attempt at irony about their bad taste. On the contrary, they were sung with the same sincerity which animated them in previous times, in their days of glory. I gathered outdated songs from all over—from France, Germany, Britain—from before the war and immediately after, and then made a selection. Arabela's preferences were decisive, because she didn't judge on aesthetic criteria. She went for what any nice girl likes when she hears a "lovely song" in the parlor, copies it on a scrap of paper, and sings it later that evening when she's sad and feels like having a cry.

Perhaps "Adelaide's Dream" and "When the Red Bill" are still hummed somewhere today. We discovered both of them in the attic of a secondhand bookstore among a stack of sheet music. One was from 1890 and the other from 1920, and we launched them in a bar for

Anglo-Saxons, with Arabela singing of Adelaide's fin de siècle dream with real feeling. Later, when we went to London for the first time, with our reputation as a European success preceding us, more for the oddness of our repertoire than our mastery of it, we had to construct an entirely English set (oh, those tender, funny evenings of cabaret in London, when the whole theater hummed along with Arabela to that silly "Venetian Moon," a lost song from 1920...), which then obliged us to construct a special set for each capital on our tour, plundering the past for old waltzes and tangos. Even I became sentimental when Arabela was rehearsing "Wien, du Stadt meiner Traume" in an awful accent for our Vienna debut—and I didn't understand half of the words.

Indeed, we were at the peak of our popularity and the illustrated theater magazines had begun to publicize how much we were earning per evening in their gossip columns, along with the anonymous love letters that arrived each morning for Arabela.

ARABELLA AND PARTNER! Blue, white, red, and green posters appeared throughout Europe like little multicolored flags planted across the continent, testifying to a victorious campaign, with our names hurrying ahead of us, on theater billboards, in tram windows, and on packets of expensive cigarettes. I loved the picture of us on the front of the program; Arabela in the foreground, drawn in crude blue—a color that suited her admirably—and me in the background, at the piano, drawn in a few black strokes that shaded my face and preserved my anonymity.

I think Arabella and Partner contained the right dose of mystery that a cabaret act needs. And, without hiding from anybody, as I had no intention of returning to my previous life, I was happy to be spared the curious attention of those who had once known me. I remained nothing more than *Partner*, which kept me out of the spotlight and the papers. Though I never admitted it to myself honestly, I was very glad that nothing was going to get back to Bucharest about it.

On several occasions we nearly got a booking back in Romania, and offers came by telegram in all our hotels when we were playing Vienna and Budapest, which would have made refusal all the harder, as I would have had trouble explaining to Arabela that I didn't want to appear there for fear of being seen by a certain woman. It was ridiculous of me, as I well knew.

When we made the film with Paramount, I had a grinding struggle with the director, who wanted both Arabela and me illuminated equally under the same bright lights. It took all my skill and stubbornness to make him see that the purity of the song and the simplicity of the image depended on my remaining in the shadows as a plain black silhouette, with just enough light to discern the play of my fingers across the keyboard for a moment before being lost against the background of the drapes. All that remained in frame was a white circle, for Arabela, who was too indifferent to it all to be troubled by the army of spotlights trained upon her.

The truth was, I was terrified by the thought of that short film making its inevitable way to Bucharest and when I thought of the spectacle being projected in a cinema to people I knew, it all seemed trivial to me. I was particularly horrified when I thought of Maria—a great lover of cinema—watching me from her seat in bewilderment, with Andrei, of course, leaning toward her and whispering casually, "That Stefan Valeriu! Told you he'd never amount to anything!"

Masterpieces are probably composed of just such tricks, as the premiere of our film received an avalanche of praise and attention, with all the critics explaining, authoritatively and in technical terms which I didn't understand, the use of light and shade in our short film. Maybe they were right, but it's hard for me to take all these aesthetic judgments seriously, knowing that all they did was hide a frivolous love affair in which, God is my witness, nothing was premeditated. Which doesn't stop me going sometimes, when I have a free evening, to a neighborhood cinema where our film is running, to see Arabela and listen to her. She is simple and moving on the screen, just as she was on the stage and at home, with her vague smile, reminiscent of a kiss.

SIX

couldn't say when exactly the little incident I'm about to relate occurred. I didn't take it seriously at the time and even today I'm not entirely certain that it had anything to do with our later breakup. One day we were talking about her old circus partners. There was sufficient detachment in our voices that the possibility of regret was not allowed to enter. Then Arabela told me straight-out, as though she'd just remembered it:

—Did you know Dik was my husband?

Of course I hadn't known. It wouldn't have crossed my mind to think it. Dik, that ageless, bald, alcoholic creature? The revelation was more comic than troubling.

—And why are you telling me this only now?

—I don't know. It never came up.

—You're extraordinary, Arabela. Extraordinary. We've been living together all this time, you go into detail about all kinds of things, every day we banter for hours about whatever crosses our minds—and it doesn't occur to you until this moment to tell me something so much more significant?

—That's the way I am, Stefan. Absentminded.

I said nothing for a moment, disarmed by the simplicity of her reply. Then I blew up:

—And why Dik? Of the four of them, why did you choose him?

—Perhaps because it was easiest with him. See? It was very hard to live the way I was, like in a family, with four men. Married to one of them, the other three had to behave. In this kind of a situation, the most important thing is to avoid love affairs and complications. And at least with Dik the idea of love couldn't enter into it—right?

Then I remembered catching Beb's look that evening at the Medrano, in the changing room, and right then I began to wonder if Arabela's decision to leave them was a more serious matter than I'd first believed, and whether her bond with them was more than just an arrangement between performers. Perhaps that boy Beb might have had an opinion on the matter. When on tour not so very much later, in a cabaret theater in Germany, I came across news of her ex-colleagues and I have to admit I was the one whom it jolted. They had performed there two weeks earlier and had since moved on to their next engagement, wherever that was. We came across their name and photograph in the theater sections of the local newspapers and I learned that their act had met with some success. They'd progressed since we'd seen them last. They weren't big stars but they put on a decent show as a warm-up act. I looked at the photographs with great interest and noted how they'd simplified their equipment, poses, and colors greatly.

—These fellows are going to do well someday, I mused.

—Maybe, said Arabela, noncommittally. It was plainly all the same to her.

I pressed on stubbornly:

—They're missing just one thing: you. Up there, on your silk swing, doing nothing, displaying yourself and smiling—you were the poetry in their trapeze act. Their useless flower. Even a director of genius wouldn't have come up with such an amazing detail.

I said this to probe her or tease her or perhaps just to exercise my old instinct for meanness. But I certainly wasn't mistaken, and, looking at those photographs, I realized that their act did lack a female presence, just as a ring might lack a gem.

Arabela heard me out, then took my arm and blew me a kiss as if to say reproachfully, Now, let's be serious and forget all that nonsense.

I don't really know why all these insignificant details are coming back to me now. I pass the time trying to remember them, the way you might try to reconstitute a game of chess you'd played. Probably they have nothing to do with what happened later and it wasn't these little incidents that caused us to break up. Rather, it was something simpler and yet harder to explain. Something that bore a striking similarity to how our love began and which might be called an affair, if such an expression could be applied to Arabela, with her childlike mentality.

Many strange things passed us by and we let them go, loving each other on the final day just as we did on the first, in the same gentle state of voluptuousness in which everything felt familiar, like the eternal taste of bread. This can go on for a year or two or ten...Or it can end at any moment. Splitting up? It happened so simply that, if I consider it very honestly, I'd find it more important to talk about the green coat Arabela wore during our first winter together or about her black dress with the yellow collar (the one that made her look much taller and made her skin pale and smooth) than to talk about how we split up.

It was in Geneva, at the beginning of September. We'd gone there to open the entertainment season in the casino's theater while two hundred paces away, at the League of Nations, Aristide Briand was opening the diplomatic season. That passionate autumn when the project of the United States of Europe was first discussed, in a frivolous celebratory atmosphere, and I'm not exaggerating if I say that Arabela's presence contributed to it greatly, as it was de rigueur for the foreign ministers to gather at nine, in their boxes, at our concert.

Dazzling mornings by the lake, the fluttering white dresses at Quai Wilson, the reporters besieging the Hotel des Bergues, the photographers lining the streets in the hope of snapping somebody famous...It was idyllic, as idyllic and relaxing as a piece of operetta.

One morning, on the quay, somebody shouted at us from behind. It was a young man who'd just jumped off a passing tram. We were on the lakefront, enjoying watching a group of English girls playing water polo. Arabela was laughing freely, the sun on her face. We turned around in surprise and at first she didn't recognize Beb, now right next to us and embarrassed by his own overexcitement at seeing her again.

—Well, Beb, said Arabela, without raising her voice. "You've changed, Beb: you're looking well. But you're still missing a button on your waistcoat. You'll fix it this evening, won't you? Do!"

Yes, Beb had certainly changed. He wasn't as pale as before, and he looked taller and fitter. He wore a gray summer suit, and in that bright September sunlight, there was something extremely juvenile in his surprise and excitement. He explained briefly that he was only in Geneva for a few days, passing through. He had to leave that evening for Montreux, where Sam and Jef were waiting for him: they had an excellent booking.

—Dik? asked Arabela.

—We lost him four months ago in Algiers and haven't heard from him since.

—And the rest of you?

—Fine. Success, money. Arabela, if only you knew how well we've been doing. I told you back then that big things were waiting for us. You remember, back when you left.

He spoke quickly, animatedly, with his hands in his pockets to stop himself from gesticulating, walking half a pace in front of us so that he could look in Arabela's eyes. He was as giddy as a schoolboy and I enjoyed it so much that I couldn't refrain from asking him, sympathetically, like a friend:

—Tell me the truth, Beb. Do you still love Arabela?

He answered straight back, lifting his chin with a certain haughtiness, but with goodwill:

—Yes!

—You're talking nonsense, the two of you, said Arabela. "Let's go and get something to eat."

Beb took the evening train for Montreux, and we went to do our usual nine o'clock show. I was very relaxed as I put on my suit. It would be nonsense to say I had any kind of presentiment. I sat at the piano and looked at Arabela and told myself, as I did every evening, that she wasn't beautiful and couldn't sing, and then accompanied her earthy voice with the same astonishment and profound peace, and it made me so melancholy, like ten slim fingers combing through memory and forgetfulness. After the show we went for a late walk along the quay. A cold wind of uncertain season blew down from the mountain, too hard to be a summer breeze, too gentle to be autumnal.

—It must be good now, up there in our room, said Arabela, leaning on the guardrail, facing the lake, squeezing my arm hard.

We went slowly up the hotel stairway, deliberately dragging out our steps, knowing that a good night awaited us, and indeed we made love then, unhurriedly, attentively, entrusting ourselves to that moment of embrace and listening to the circles of silence expanding about us in the dark.

I think that even the slightest misunderstanding that might still have remained between our bodies must have dissipated then in the closeness of that night. In the darkness, she lay like a little sleepy animal, and her smile was warm. Perhaps that was why I wasn't shocked the next morning when, as I was waiting for her in the lobby, I saw her coming down the stairs toward me, beckoning me with a wave, and she said, as though asking what time it was:

—What would you say, Stefan, if I ran off with Beb?

—I don't know, sweetheart. I think it would be complicated, with the theater here. We have a contract...

—I'd sort that out...

— All right! Let's try then!

I accompanied her to the station after lunch. All she took was a single, small case she could carry by hand. The rest of her things were being sent on. We made small talk until the train came, then we shook hands undramatically, with complete mutual understanding.

—Put your coat on if it gets cold in the evening, Stefan. It gets very cool down on the lakeshore!

It was five, getting on toward evening. I walked into town and bought the papers on the way to see what had happened that morning at the League of Nations. There had been heated debates.

MIHAIL SEBASTIAN was born in Romania in 1907 as Iosif Mendel Hechter. He worked as a lawyer and writer until anti-Semitic legislation forced him to abandon his public career. Having survived the war and the Holocaust, he was killed in a road accident in early 1945 as he was crossing the street to teach his first class. His long-lost diary, *Journal 1935–1944: The Fascist Years*, was published to great acclaim in the late 1990s. His novel *For Two Thousand Years* was published in English in 2016.

PHILIP Ó CEALLAIGH is a writer as well as a translator. In 2006 he won the Rooney Prize for Irish Literature. His two short-story collections, *Notes from a Turkish Whorehouse* and *The Pleasant Light of Day*, were short-listed for the Frank O'Connor International Short Story Award. He lives in Bucharest.